The Seductive Temptress

Fate of the Worthingtons

Laura A. Barnes

To Bill – Thank you for your unrelenting faith

The Seductive Temptress

Chapter One

NOEL WORTHINGTON FELT THE first crack of her face breaking into a hundred tiny pieces when she smiled serenely at another well-wisher. With each smile, the dreaded emotion of sorrow stabbed her in the heart. She fought back a fresh wave of tears that hovered behind her eyelids, ready to drop at a moment's notice. She wished to steal away to her bedchamber. However, she refused to abandon her sister during her blush of happiness.

Even when it should have been hers.

Her younger sister had married before her and with undo haste. It had set the gossip mill swapping rumors on the reason for Maggie's wedding—and to a gentleman few had heard of, no less. The rumors floated from one ear to the next, because it should have been Noel's wedding to Lord Ravencroft they attended. However, her intended had disappeared, abandoning her to the masses and with not a single explanation as to why.

Oh, the obvious deception of his involvement with Lady Langdale and her threat to destroy Noel's family was enough to cause her brother Reese to withdraw his support of their engagement. However, Reese had never withdrawn his support. He was furious with how the circumstances had played out, but he wanted to keep Ravencroft close. So he had agreed they could still marry. After all, Ravencroft was Maggie's new husband's half-brother.

Noel refused to listen to the story of how the gentlemen had infiltrated themselves into their family. She didn't want to believe the bond they held was false. Noel's heart had already committed itself to a lifetime of loving Gregory Ravencroft.

However, the proof of his deception proved true with each passing day he remained absent. Why did he stay away? Did he not love her as he had declared? If so, he would've arrived for the wedding. The longer he stayed away, the more difficult it would be for him to admit to his wrongdoings, and her love would slowly wither away.

Noel watched Maggie and her husband, Crispin Dracott, dance to a waltz across the ballroom floor. The love shining from her sister's eyes helped warm the cold seeping into Noel's heart. When the corner of her lips lifted this time, it was genuine. Her only shining happiness was for her sister. Dracott was the perfect match for Maggie. He complemented her curious sense of adventure with a patience none of them had been able to achieve.

With one last glance at the happy couple, Noel moved to stand behind a set of columns. She needed a moment to herself from all the glances of pity. As much as she longed to retire to her bedchamber, she wouldn't ruin Maggie's day with her sadness. She wished Ravencroft were here, not only to ease the burden of the meddlesome questions but to hold her hand while she shared in the joy with their family and friends. Instead, loneliness wrapped her in a cloak of despair.

"Why in the hell did he not show?" Reese growled.

"Dracott said it was for the best he stayed away," Graham explained.

Graham was Noel's other brother who owned a detective agency that Dracott worked for. It was how Dracott had become acquainted with their family. Graham had assigned Dracott to watch over Maggie at the functions they attended because their sister had the dreadful habit of wandering where she shouldn't. He had faked a title to deceive their family. But Noel held no ill feelings for him because of the love he held for Maggie.

Reese continued with his irritation for the missing lord. "Best for whom? Himself? I thought he cared for Noel, but his actions have proven otherwise."

"He is in a drunken stupor. His presence today would've given more room for gossip. Not to mention the effect it would have on Noel," Graham stated.

"Can you not see the effect it is having on Noel already?" Reese asked.

Noel pressed closer to the columns to overhear her brothers' conversation. As usual, Graham was oblivious to how Ravencroft's behavior affected her. And Reese was only aware because his wife, Evelyn, had confided in him. She shook her head at the misguided way her brothers regarded her feelings, but at least they cared. It was more than some people had. Ravencroft's actions were proof of that.

Graham appeared confused. "She seems well. I have seen her smiling and visiting with the guests all day."

Reese glared at Graham. "Only because our mother has instilled in her how to keep up appearances. Stare into her eyes and you will see the sadness deep within. Our dear sister holds herself together with dignity but is falling apart inside."

Any other time, Noel would smirk at her brother's insight into her emotions. But he hit too close to the target for her to find humor in his words. Perhaps she sold Reese short on the attention he paid her. She understood Graham's distraction.

Usually, he was the first one to tease a smile onto her face, but now he faced tremendous pressure to secure the capture of Lady Langdale and her thievery ring. Now, with the risk placed on their family, it only added to his drive to destroy Lady Langdale.

"How can I help her?" Graham asked.

"Tomorrow morning, you and I will pay Lord Ravencroft a visit and make him understand his obligation to our sister. I will not allow him to leave Noel at the altar. Since he started this game, we will make sure he finishes it," Reese threatened.

"Is that fair to Noel?"

"Sometimes life is not about fairness. It is about fulfilling a promise made. He made a promise to marry Noel and spent the season portraying a doting fiancé. Also, he tricked Noel into believing he loved her. Therefore, he will spend a lifetime proving the truth of his declarations," Reese explained.

Graham shook his head. "I thought after the length of your marriage to Evelyn, you would've gained a better perspective on emotions. But you remain as clueless as ever. You cannot force matters as sensitive as this. You must coerce them with a gentleness they are unaware of being subjected to."

Reese scoffed. "As always, you talk nonsense."

Graham laughed. "Once again, I must prove you wrong."

Her brothers moved away, preventing Noel from hearing the rest of their conversation. However, she had heard enough. While she loved her brothers dearly, she didn't want their interference. If Reese went to Ravencroft and issued his demands, it would only send Ravencroft fleeing. While her fiancé kept her in the dark about his true character, she understood how much he valued his pride. He wouldn't allow another gentleman to threaten him. Nor did Noel want Ravencroft to return on those terms. If he didn't return on his own accord, then she had no use for him. No matter how much her heart cried otherwise.

Noel was more determined than ever to confront Ravencroft before her brothers did. Her gaze swept the ballroom for anyone to help her sneak away to Ravencroft's home. But she couldn't trust anyone not to inform Reese of her plans. He had stated how unsafe it was for them outside their home and only to leave under the protection of the guards assigned to them. Noel racked her mind for ways to leave undetected. When her gaze landed on Maggie, the perfect solution sprang her into action.

She inched out of the drawing room, glancing over her shoulder to see if anyone noticed her escape. The guests mingled with each other, while the servants bustled around, carrying trays of champagne and hors d'oeuvres. Noel hurried up the stairs and snuck into Maggie's bedchamber. She opened the sewing chest and dug to the bottom of her sister's hiding spot. When her fingers brushed across the fabric, she gave a yank. A pair of trousers and an old shirt of Graham's appeared. Noel's face lit up at how easily her plan fell into place.

She gathered the clothing and stepped across the hall into her bedchamber. After locking the door behind her, she tossed the clothes onto the bed. Noel's heartbeat quickened when someone knocked on the door. She hurried to the bed and slid the clothes under the pillow. She couldn't afford to get caught so early with her plan.

"Yes," she called out.

"It's Mama, dear."

Noel took a deep breath to calm her nerves. She opened the door, pasting on her last smile for the evening. "I am sorry for leaving so early."

Her mother drew her into a hug, and Noel wanted to cling to her and cry out her injustice. However, she wanted Mama to enjoy Maggie's special day. She must hurry if she wanted to escape before the celebration ended.

"It is understandable, my dear. I only wanted to check on you. If you like, I can sit with you for a spell."

"I have not slept well lately and wish to retire for the evening. You must return and enjoy the celebration," Noel fibbed.

"I can stay until you fall asleep," Mama offered.

Noel's gaze drifted toward the bed. "No. I wish to be alone with my thoughts."

Mama looked disappointed, and Noel feared she might overrule her wishes and stay. Her family thought she needed to be coddled during this time. She grew weary of pretending her problems would resolve themselves when she really wanted to scream from the rafters. But it wasn't her mother's fault and she wouldn't take out her frustration on her.

"But you can help me get ready for bed."

Mama smiled. Her mother only wanted to feel needed, and Noel needed her mother's comfort now more than ever. Mama turned her around and unbuttoned her gown, helping her into a nightdress. Noel picked out the simplest one to pull off when her mother left. Mama settled them on the divan and brushed out Noel's hair. With each stroke of the brush, Noel fought with her guilty conscience for what she planned to do.

"Sometimes love must undergo a traumatic event to test the strength of its bond," Mama murmured.

"What if it breaks the bond?" Noel whispered.

Mama laid the hairbrush to the side and pulled Noel back into her embrace. "Then one of two things will happen."

"And those are?"

"Either you will realize it was never love to begin with or you will fight to repair the tear in that bond." Mama placed a kiss on Noel's head before rising. She set the brush on the vanity, picked up Noel's clothes, and placed them on a chair for the maid to clear in the morning. "Good night, my dear."

"Night, Mama."

Her mother paused at the door and focused her gaze on the pillows. She stared at them before smiling wistfully at Noel. Then she left, making no comment on what she had observed. Noel glanced at the bed in panic. Had her mother seen the garments? However, nothing looked out of place. An eerie sense settled over Noel that her mother had figured out her plans. Noel shook her head. Her only explanation was that her guilt had led her to imagine it.

What other explanation could there be?

Chapter Two

NOEL WAITED FOR A while before changing her clothes again. She tore off her nightdress and pulled on the disguise once she realized her mother wouldn't return. When she wiggled into them, Noel wondered how Maggie had ever found the trousers comfortable to wear. The linen shirt differed vastly from the silk she adorned her body with. She rubbed her hand across her stomach, soothing her sensitive skin from the coarse material.

After walking back and forth across the rug, Noel realized she couldn't adjust to how the trousers hugged her buttocks and rubbed against her core. Should she wear drawers with these things? If so, she didn't see how. It was most scandalous how the fabric clung to her like a second skin. Also provocative. Noel grew warm at how intimate the garments were.

However, she had no alternative disguise that would guarantee her escape. She must leave if she wanted to make her demands to Ravencroft before Reese. She moved to the bed and arranged the pillows to appear as if she slept under the covers, nodding with satisfaction at her results. Then she moved to the windows and unlatched them. She glanced at the trellis, then the ground. She had never attempted to climb on the trellis before and hoped it was as sturdy as it appeared. If not, then her family would discover her absence earlier than she wanted them to. One aspect that worked to her advantage was how her bedroom faced the side of the house, where no one would notice her escape.

"Here goes nothing. Wish yourself luck, Noel," she muttered to herself.

She swung from the window to the trellis, and with trembling hands, she lowered herself to the bottom. Noel moved with an ease unfamiliar to her, one that felt like second nature. Noel didn't ponder why and jumped from the last rung. She pressed herself against the house, hoping to go unnoticed when she overheard some gentlemen talking. They were the men Reese had hired from Griffen Kincaid's security firm to guard their home. When she peeked around the corner, they were moving in the opposite direction.

Noel stole through the garden to the alleyway. She found the secret entrance, slid through, and kept to the shadows as she moved along. After she took a few steps, something pulled at her hair, bringing her to a stop. She held her breath, afraid someone had caught her sneaking away. When no one spoke, she looked over her shoulder to see her hair had gotten caught in the hedge. Noel tugged her hair loose and continued on. In her hurry to leave, she had forgotten to hide her locks underneath a cap. Only two more houses separated her from Ravencroft's townhome.

At least she didn't have to travel across London to reach him. Noel wasn't brave enough to take that risk. How Maggie had, she never understood. When she reached the back gate to Ravencroft's home, the house sat in darkness. Perhaps Dracott had misinformed Graham, and Ravencroft had recovered and decided to attend the wedding after all. Noel almost ran back home when she saw a flame shining outside.

Noel opened the gate and paused when it creaked, waiting for Ravencroft to acknowledge an intruder. However, when he didn't make any demands, she drew closer and noticed Ravencroft smoking a cigar in between drinking from a bottle. He swayed in a drunken stupor while muttering incoherently. His behavior was unlike anything she had witnessed from him before. She'd never seen him indulge in alcohol around her, unless it was a drink he shared with her brothers. Oh, she was aware of how he liked to smoke cigars, but the air held a lingering stench, indicating it wasn't his first one of the evening.

A small lantern rested on a table near Ravencroft. The glow offered her a look at him, and she gasped at his haggard expression. Wrinkled clothes clung to his frame, and his hair stood on end as if he had raked his hands through it multiple times. This wasn't the gentleman who courted her with devotion for the entire ton to see. No. This was a gentleman tormented by the demons of his past, who tortured himself with his regrets and hoped to soothe them with alcohol. She knew the outcome if he continued on this path. Noel's father had behaved in the same manner, and she understood the aftermath of the destruction it would cause if she didn't stop him. She refused to allow him to ruin their future.

"You should have worn a cap," Ravencroft slurred before taking a drag of his cigar.

Noel ran her hands over her hair at his disapproval.

He swung the bottle out with his finger, twirling it in the air. "And you need to practice on your stealth. You are a bit noisy in your attempt to go undetected."

Ravencroft lifted the bottle to his lips and took a long swallow. He swayed on his feet but caught himself in time. He tried to focus his gaze on the object of his misery, but he kept seeing two of her. When his vision cleared to only seeing one of her, he took note of her vulnerability. Noel's defensive stance displayed how she wished to tear into him, but her quivering lips showed how his harsh comments had injured her pride. He savored another drink, hoping it would give him the courage to insult her so she would return home. He must destroy any feelings she held for him. It was for her own good, and the only way to protect her from the dangers lurking beyond the shadows. It was foolish of her to come after him. He had never thought her one for rash decisions, but her actions this evening implied otherwise.

"You should leave," he demanded.

Noel bristled under Ravencroft's harsh words. If he thought to send her away by pretending his disinterest, then he should've glanced in a mirror. Because his longing gaze showed her how much she meant to him. It beckoned her closer to ease his burden. Oh, how she wanted to. But first, she needed him to understand how she wouldn't allow him to control her.

She swung her hip to the side and landed her fist atop it. "Perhaps it was my intention to go undetected. Maybe, just maybe, I wished for my fiancé to take notice of me." Noel snarled the last bit.

Ravencroft flicked his cigar, stalked across to Noel, and yanked her into his arms with a glare. "You are a fool to risk your life for the likes of me."

Noel wanted nothing more than to soften in his arms. However, she must make her point clear to him and not allow him to scare her away. Instead, she would annoy him with her responses and force him to react where they could discuss this drama like two reasonable adults.

Her shoulders lifted in indifference. "Mmm. Perhaps."

Ravencroft growled at her foolishness. He needed to teach her a lesson about what happened to a lady who wandered in the dark. His head lowered to whisper a scandalous suggestion in her ear when the fresh scent of lilacs on a warm summer day flooded his senses. The fragrance shifted his attention into wanting to give Noel a sweet kiss. To savor her innocence and let it invade his dark soul. Would her lips hold the same sweetness as her soul? Or would it strike a flame and burn him fiercely?

Noel softened at the desire burning in Ravencroft's gaze. It stated his intentions. Her toes curled, anticipating her first kiss. Would he be gentle? Or would he ravish her lips with a passion out of control? Either way, it would finally happen. She had dreamt of this day since he first asked her to dance. She thought he would have by now, considering their engagement. Instead, he offered her his devotion by his gentlemanly attendance at every function and charmed her family. He played a gentleman to the highest esteem. As frustrating as it was, it was also something Noel admired about Ravencroft.

She had lied to Maggie about sharing kisses with Ravencroft. They were only figments of her imagination. She dreamt every night of his warm embrace and the kisses he ravished from her lips. How was she to admit to her younger sister that no gentleman, even her own fiancé, had ever attempted to kiss her after she had watched Maggie and Dracott share a kiss?

Ravencroft watched Noel's eyes grow heavy with desire. Her eyelids lowered, and her lips formed a soft pucker. Hell! That was the exact spot he stood in at this moment. The devil in him pestered him to take what the lady offered. To kiss her innocence away and tempt her into sin. A simple enough act since Noel offered herself to him so willingly. How easy it would be for him to tempt her every desire to his benefit. To sweep her into his arms, lay her before the fire, and unleash his passion on her.

She didn't realize how tempting of a package she displayed herself in the snug trousers that molded to her every curve. Her unbound breasts pressed against his chest. With one swoop, he could discard her shirt and feast upon them. Were her nipples a light pink or were they the color of berries? Either way, his mouth watered in anticipation of sucking them between his lips to savor the unique flavor. He wanted to hitch her leg over his hip and press his cock into her core. To make her aware of the danger she had placed herself in with her visit.

With a deep moan, he released her and drowned his desires with another drink, instead of kissing her. He stalked away, not even giving her the courtesy of helping her regain her balance. He must remove himself from her presence before he fulfilled every fantasy he held of them together. If not, Ravencroft would scandalize Noel by sticking his cock inside her with the tree against her back. He would press her into the bark and listen to her screams of pleasure filling the air.

Ravencroft had sunk into a dark hell, and he didn't wish to ruin Noel. If she came anywhere near him, he didn't know if he could hold himself to behave like a gentleman. He had kept himself reined in throughout their courtship, but now he was unsure of his ability to remain indifferent with his life engulfed in turmoil. Noel represented everything he desired but could never have. He had fooled himself into believing otherwise. However, he had awakened to his foolishness once his mother reappeared and threatened to expose his secrets.

"Return to your home, princess," Ravencroft snarled.

It was how he viewed Noel. She held the quality of a gracious lady who only displayed her intelligence when needed. Her simple thoughts fooled most people. However, they were anything but simple. He had learned early on after he started courting her how unique she was. She allowed only those close to her to appreciate the intellect of her thoughts. Noel fooled everyone else, leaving them vulnerable to her cleverness.

Noel defied him. "No."

"Yes," Ravencroft growled.

She took a step toward him. "I deserve an explanation for your disappearance."

Ravencroft scoffed. "My lady, I owe you nothing."

Noel stomped her foot. "We are engaged. You will fulfill the promise you made me."

Ravencroft's dark chuckle sent a shiver along her spine. Instead of answering her, he took another drink from the bottle, then he walked over to her again. Noel trembled, not from fear but from how she yearned for his touch. He had almost kissed her before. Would he fulfill her dreams and kiss her now? Instead of drawing her in his arms again, he walked in a slow circle around her. At first she kept turning with him but grew dizzy as he continued the act.

When he passed her, she noticed the interest in his eyes. They kept sweeping up and down her body, much to her delight. On his next pass, he stepped closer, and the heat radiating off his body warmed her. Ravencroft stopped right behind her and paused. He never touched her, but he didn't need to. His closeness wrapped her in a seductive embrace.

Ravencroft closed his eyes, willing himself to keep his hands off her. Her body trembled each time he passed around her. Noel wanted him to caress her. Ravencroft knew how a lady reacted when the desire she held went unattended. Soft sighs would whisper between her lips without her realizing it. Her tongue would wet her lips to prepare for a kiss. While her body would soften to having the one she desire so close, it was strung taut, waiting to have her every desire fulfilled.

Noel wanted him.

"I do not have to fulfill anything I do not wish to," Ravencroft whispered near her ear.

Noel shuddered at the warm breath across her ear. It took a moment for her to understand his words. She spun around to confront him, but once again Ravencroft strode away. She moved after him and grabbed at his arm.

"You act like a drunken fool," Noel berated him.

He shook off her hand. "I may be drunk, but I am no fool. You are the fool to throw yourself at me."

"Fool? Throw? You?" Noel sputtered.

Ravencroft's laughter grew more cynical. "Yes."

Noel took a deep breath to draw in her temper, but she actually wanted to scream her fury at him to see reason. But she had learned at a young age from watching her parents argue that words spoken in anger only drove a deeper wedge and harmed the innocent. If she laid the foundation for this behavior, this evening, it would set a precedent for every argument they would ever share.

"I see you are unable to reach clarity because of your intolerance to the spirits you consume. So I will save this conversation for when you are sober. Perhaps then we can reach a compromise. For now, I wish you a good evening and my sympathy for the headache you will endure on the morrow." With a nod, she turned and started for home.

Ravencroft couldn't believe the audacity of this lady. For every argument he gave her to steer clear of him, she refused to see reason and fought him to continue their relationship. Why? Did she worry it would ruin her chance of securing another match? She couldn't possibly hold any sort of feelings for him since she had never expressed them before, only preened over his attention whenever her family or friends were around. They may enjoy each other's company, but not once had she ever shown him she desired more. Had he misjudged how she felt? Either way, it no longer mattered. He refused to risk her life for his wishful fantasies.

He raised the bottle to his lips for another drink, but found it empty. Ravencroft threw the bottle against the house after his frustrations took hold. The glass shattering echoed into the night, causing Noel to pause at the gate. If she thought he would allow her to leave without making himself clear, then she would soon learn to never walk away from him without his permission.

His long strides ate up the distance between them. He wrapped his arms around her waist and threw her over his shoulder. The drumming of her fists on his back didn't break his return to the house. With one arm securing her legs against his chest, he threw the door open to his study and stormed inside. He dropped Noel into a chair and moved behind his desk. Ravencroft needed to place distance between them because his need to kiss her was stronger than ever after holding her in his arms.

Damn her. She smelt like lilacs all over, and now the intoxicating scent of her filled his study.

He sat up in his chair with authority and held his arms out. "The floor is yours to speak, my lady. State whatever is on your mind so you can be on your way." Ravencroft's offer held his mockery of the situation.

Noel was beyond shocked at his brutal treatment of her person. How dare he throw her about like a sack of potatoes? Yet the strength of his arms as he held her to him sparked her desire back to life.

She shook her head to clear her thoughts. She was furious with him, and there was nothing desirable about his behavior. Not one single act.

Noel jumped to her feet and pointed her finger at Ravencroft. "Your behavior is atrocious. How dare you treat me with such callous disregard."

He leaned back with a smirk. "And how should I treat you? Do you wish to hear more false promises and whispers of my utter devotion?"

The look of disbelief on Noel's face gutted him. His questions made it appear as if his attention toward her the past few months had been an act to draw her attention away from his deception. It was anything but. He had meant every compliment he spoke. However, he refused to allow her to believe otherwise.

When she didn't answer him, he knew what he must do to drive her away. He had hoped to avoid it because it would affect him more than her. However, she left him with no other options.

He must kiss her.

But not an ordinary kiss. No. It wouldn't be gentle. Or sweet. He must show her how he only meant to trifle with her. To steal her innocence and leave her with a scandal to deal with. He had no other choice but to frighten her away.

One kiss. That was it. Only one. He would kiss her. Whisper a scandalous proposition. Scare her away. It was as simple as that.

How had she mistaken Ravencroft's affections all these months? Was she so gullible to believe everything a gentleman said to her? His actions showed proof of it. She stared at him, searching for any sign that he had lied. However, he sat relaxed with not a care in the world.

When he rose from his chair and prowled toward her, Noel stood dumbfounded about how to react. She should run home and cry over her heartache. Yet her curiosity about his intentions kept her still. His gaze held a determination she had never seen. Before she realized his intent, he drew her against him and ravished her lips.

His kiss wasn't kind. Nor was it frightening. It was powerful. Addictive. All-consuming. His lips slashed against hers, demanding her capitulation. He never coaxed her lips apart but invaded her mouth with his demands. Each stroke of his tongue against hers ordered her to submit to his desire. Noel whimpered. He stole her breath away with one kiss after another.

It wasn't how she had dreamed of her first kiss. She held the thoughts of a foolish girl who imagined their first kiss would be a gentle show of affection. She'd thought birds would sing and a rainbow would appear. Never in her wildest fantasies did she imagine the darkness pulling them into a raging passion, leaving behind victims at the mercy of their desires. No. Her expectations were from a girl; instead Ravencroft granted her a kiss meant for a woman he craved.

Ravencroft plunged his hands through Noel's hair and gripped her head to his. His desire was out of his control. Just as he knew it would be if he ever placed his lips upon hers. One kiss turned to two. To three. To more than he could count. Each time he came up for air, his hunger pulled him back in to devour her. Her soft whimpers after each swipe of their tongues only ignited his need. When her hands curled around his arms and she met him kiss for kiss, he welcomed his demise.

There was nothing sweeter on this earth than the taste of Noel. He savored her disappointment, her wonder, her curiosity, her fury each time their lips passed over each other. He must stop this madness before he took her upon his desk. Her eagerness when he changed the dynamic of their kisses only showed him how she would be a pleasure to bed.

Noel moaned. "Oh, Gregory."

When she called him by his name, it was as if someone threw a bucket of water over him. He had taken the kiss too far and led her to believe they shared an intimate moment. He must dissuade her belief.

Ravencroft pulled his lips away from her mouth and seared a path of kisses along her neck. "What do you say, love, shall you spread your thighs open upon my desk or would you prefer wrapping your legs around my waist as I pound into you against the wall?"

The scandalous suggestions Ravencroft whispered both shocked and stirred her curiosity. Were those options even a possibility? Before the full implications of his statement awoke Noel to his crudity, his hand slipped up her shirt and cupped her breast. It wasn't a gentle grip, but one to show her of his intentions. When his fingers tightened around her nipple, Noel's knees weakened. There were no words to describe his sensuous touch.

When his comment didn't shock her into slapping his face, he proceeded with his seduction. Surely she would voice her objections soon. She had to. His sanity had forgotten the differences between right and wrong. And there was no doubt his every action was definitely wrong. But oh, it felt so right. His cock throbbed in his trousers for release. If she didn't slap him soon, he would wrap his lips around her perk nipple. He enjoyed how, with one touch, it tightened into a hard bud between his fingers. If he slipped his hand down her trousers, would he discover Noel wet for him?

He slid a finger back and forth inside the placket of her trousers just enough to grab her attention. "Is your cunny wet for me, Noel? Will it taste as sweet as your kisses?"

Noel's whimpers ceased and her hands dropped from his arms at his vulgar questions. Ravencroft wanted to breathe a sigh of relief that he had stopped the madness. However, he must continue since she hadn't moved away from him. And until she did, he couldn't relent.

His hand dipped lower, brushing across her curls. He didn't dare venture any lower or else he would become a doomed man who was powerless to stop. "Do you want me to stroke your heat? Or perhaps you wish for my tongue to heighten your pleasure."

Noel gasped and stepped back. "You are so crude."

Ravencroft leered at her, making her aware of what he desired. With each step she inched back toward the door, he took a step toward her. He tore his shirt over his head and started on the buttons on the placket of his trousers.

She held out a hand. "Stop."

"Why, my love? I thought you wanted me to fulfill my promise."

Noel shook her head rapidly from side to side. He misconstrued her visit, turning it into something vulgar. This wasn't the man she had fallen in love with. This was a stranger. Had she ever loved Ravencroft to begin with? Or had she only loved the idea of falling in love?

"Not this way," Noel cried.

Ravencroft's chest rumbled with laughter. "Ah, love, why not? I am more than willing." He glanced down at the front of himself.

Noel followed his gaze and noticed the fullness of his trousers. When he caught her staring, he stepped closer. A warm blush spread across her cheeks, and an invisible force pushed her to touch him. Her fingers dipped in and out, tracing the ridges of his muscles.

He grabbed her hand, tightening his hold. Each time he thought he had scared her away, she fooled him by responding to his demands. He would ruin her if his next attempt didn't send her running away. He loosened his hold and guided her hand along his chest, leading her lower, across his stomach.

Ravencroft leaned over and placed a kiss on the corner of her lips. "Just a little lower, my dear, and you can help ease the ache consuming my soul. You need only to wrap your fingers around my cock and tug a few times." He settled their hands over his cock. "Unless you prefer to get on your knees and use your mouth instead."

Noel's eyes widened. She yanked her hand away and opened her mouth to call him out on his coarse behavior, but no words came out. She only looked like a guppy opening and closing her mouth. When his eyes darkened into an upcoming storm, Noel reacted the only way she could.

She fled.

Chapter Three

N OEL FLEW ALONG THE path back to her townhome. Ravencroft's taunting laughter followed on her heels. She couldn't run fast enough. How come it took longer to return home than it took to arrive at Ravencroft's? She leaned against a fence to catch her breath, glancing over her shoulder to make sure he didn't follow her.

Her hand trembled against her lips. The press of his lips as he kissed her still lingered. Its possessive hold over her senses dominated her thoughts. How could a simple kiss hold the power to make her forget her inhibitions? She never in her wildest imaginations expected to partake in such sinful explorations. Or even want to.

Instead of shocking her, Ravencroft had only awakened her curiosity. With each scandalous suggestion, he taunted her in his attempt to scare her away. Instead, they only turned her into a wanton hussy wanting him to show her how they were possible.

Noel's breathing quickened at the thought of his last provocative remark before she fled. Her hand tingled from touching the strength of his passion and itched from wanting to indulge in his taunt. As much as he had attempted to shock Noel, her actions shocked her even more.

Her wanton thoughts distracted her from the danger lurking in the night's darkness.

When she heard footsteps coming up behind her, she thought Ravencroft had followed her to finish what he started. However, she misjudged the danger she was in.

Someone lifted Noel over their shoulder. The first clue that it wasn't Ravencroft was an overwhelming stench clung to the individual. Her head slammed into a steel back, while beefy hands locked her legs to a chest. Before she could belt out a scream, someone else smothered her mouth and nose with a foul-smelling rag. She squirmed and pounded on her abductor's back until she sank into a dark abyss. The last thing she remembered was her kidnappers bragging about their heist.

"That was easier than I thought. Why do you suppose she wanders in the dark on her wedding night?"

"Who knows with these toffs. Hurry we must before someone spots us."

They believed they had captured Maggie.

Ravencroft stumbled outside after Noel. Her touch had intoxicated him more than the whiskey he drank. Her kisses burned a path of desire straight to his cock. While he had toyed with her to chase her away, his body ached for them to continue. However, it was for the best that she ran. He only followed her to assuage his guilt that she returned home unharmed. It was foolish of her to wander around in the dark.

Where in the hell were her brothers? His brother, Crispin, had mentioned how Reese Worthington had hired guards to watch over their townhome. However, they secured the home poorly if Noel was able to sneak away. If he was in his right mind, he would storm Worthington's townhome and demand to know why they had left Noel unprotected.

But even in his drunken state, he knew a warm reception wouldn't welcome him. Nor did he wish to ruin his brother's wedding celebration. It was reprehensible of him not to attend the nuptials, and tomorrow he would regret his actions. He justified his reasoning with the excuse of his unstable temperament. Crispin had stated he understood. However, after Noel's visit, he knew his fiancée didn't hold the same opinion as his brother.

No. She was quite furious. He never imagined she possessed the capability for such fierce emotion. It changed the dynamics of their relationship. He wasn't a fool. Reese Worthington would never allow him to back out of the betrothal. Crispin had even stated so earlier today. Which left Ravencroft wondering if Noel was a suitable choice for a bride. He wanted a manageable wife after watching his father's torturous marriage to his mother. He swore when he married, it would be to a lady who never displayed a temper and who expressed herself with pleasantries.

However, the lady who had called on him this evening was anything but serene.

Yet her very attitude this evening had inflamed his senses. She left him twisted in knots about her opinion of him, not to mention how his body ached to finish what they started. Why did he fool himself into believing he would find contentment with a pleasant wife who never argued with him? Not when he could have a passionate wife who kept his desires stroked with the most delicious kisses.

Ravencroft reached the gate and paused. Where was he headed? He shook his head to recall what had prompted him to leave. He grabbed at the gate as he swayed back and forth. Oh yes, now he remembered. Noel. He started off down the lane after her. Once he neared the Worthington townhome and didn't come across Noel, he figured she had made it home without harm. So he returned home.

After propping his feet on a stool, he relaxed back into his favorite leather chair in front of the fire. He refused to drink anything else and wash away the taste of Noel's kiss. Hell, her kisses stimulated his fantasies. He closed his eyes as he recalled her delectable form encased in the snug trousers. She made for a tempting package he wished to unwrap.

Their engagement held promise after all.

"Dracott warned us," Worth muttered in disgust.

Worthington looked around the study with annoyance. They had walked into Ravencroft's home as if it were their own. After knocking repeatedly with no answer, they had let themselves in. After searching for him, they had run into a maid who explained the lack of servants. She had directed them toward Ravencroft's study and apologized for the state of the room.

Worthington lifted an eyebrow in disbelief. "I am left with the opinion that he understated his brother's condition."

Worth chuckled. "Who would have thought Ravencroft would overindulge?"

Worthington picked up an empty bottle. "It does not come as a surprise considering how he deceived our family."

Worth stepped toward the open door leading to the garden. He glanced outside, noting the broken glass. He picked up a piece and showed his brother. "Do you imagine he had trouble?"

Before Worthington responded, Ravencroft mumbled in his sleep, "Noel. Noel. Come back, love, I wish for another taste of your . . ."

Worthington growled and turned a bright red, striding over to Ravencroft with his hands tightened into fists. Worth dropped the glass, rushing toward his brother. However, he wasn't quick enough. Worthington grabbed Ravencroft by his shirt and shook him. Ravencroft's eyes popped open, and his arms struck out to protect himself. One of his hands smacked Worthington across the cheek, which fueled the earl's temper. Worthington swung his fist out and connected with Ravencroft's eye. Before he took another swing, Worth pulled his brother away. Worthington dropped his hold on Ravencroft, and the lord fell to the floor.

"What in the hell?" Ravencroft slurred.

Worthington took a step back toward him. "He is still sloshed."

Ravencroft opened his mouth to defend himself. However, he decided against it when Worth shook his head to stay silent. Also, he was wise enough not to argue with the earl after his brutal treatment. His head already pounded like the devil stomping in anger and wouldn't tolerate any more agony this morning.

He pulled himself off the floor and slumped back into his chair. He hoped their visit wouldn't last long. Ravencroft needed a hot bath and a bed. And not in any particular order. His body protested from his evening of abuse.

A memory flashed of pleasure he had enjoyed in a lady's arms. Apparently, last night wasn't too particularly dreadful.

"What do I owe this pleasure?" Ravencroft drawled.

His brother had warned him of their visit. It was the very reason he had picked up the bottle of whiskey. He knew they wanted answers to his involvement with Lady Langdale.

Securing his livelihood was within his grasp if he married Noel Worthington. However, when his mother reappeared, she had threatened to ruin his chance at happiness and had drawn Crispin and him into Lady L's web of destruction.

Now, Worthington arrived to force his agenda. If he didn't marry Noel, then Worthington would make it difficult for him to find any bride. There was no need for Worthington to issue his warnings because Ravencroft understood his duty. Either marry Noel or Worthington would ruin him in every way possible.

"Have you been inappropriate with our sister?" Worthington growled.

"May I inquire as to when I would've had the opportunity to do so? Our visits always have a chaperone present," Ravencroft explained.

As Ravencroft denied Worthington's suggestion, a warm sensation overwhelmed him. He recalled flashes of a stolen memory filled with kisses and moans of pleasure. Noel whispering his name while he filled his hands with her breasts. Even her scent of lilacs teased the air surrounding him.

"Then why did you . . . ?" Worthington started.

Worth slapped his hand over his brother's shoulder to stop him. "Probably just the ramblings of a gentleman's dream. After all, he is engaged to Noel."

Worth attempted to soothe his brother's temper by explaining how a gentleman's thoughts ran when they were engaged. While it was a sensitive subject, Worthington must understand Ravencroft's discomfort. The man wasn't a saint. He needed to get their visit back on course, and talking about a man's fantasies about their sister wasn't an appropriate option to continue with.

"We missed you at Maggie and Crispin's wedding yesterday," Worth said.

"As you can see, I had more pressing matters to attend to," Ravencroft quipped.

Worthington growled. "We can see."

"I am sure it was a lovely affair. Blushing bride and all. Is your visit to guarantee your other sister will suffer the same outcome?" Ravencroft asked.

Worthington advanced on Ravencroft again. "Suffer?"

Worth sighed and pulled his brother back. "Gentlemen, can we have an amicable discussion? Please."

Ravencroft swept his hand out for them to take a seat. He wouldn't have Worthington intimidate him in his own home. Once they sat, he straightened in his chair. His body might suffer the aftereffects of his indulgence, but his mind remained sharp. "What is it you wish to discuss? Noel? Lady Langdale? My mother? Crispin? Where shall we start?"

"Dracott has already briefed us on his relationship with you, your mother, and Lady Langdale. We have come to ask for your help to bring Lady L to justice," Worth explained.

Ravencroft nodded. "I already told Dracott I will. In which, I am sure he already informed you. So shall we proceed with the discussion of my engagement to Noel? Are you here to force the marriage or demand I withdraw my offer?"

Worthington glared at Ravencroft's offhanded behavior, and he wanted to laugh at his reaction. He always portrayed himself as an amiable fellow, and his behavior today confused the earl. It wasn't one he was proud of, but he reverted to this behavior when he dealt with the uncertainties of life. Once upon a time, he had been a good-natured fellow until his mother sank her claws into him. Then he had learned to constantly change his character to leave one wondering who he actually was. How he longed for the days when he could just be himself. However, those days were in the past, never to be experienced again.

"Force is such a harsh word," Worth stated.

Ravencroft cleared his throat at the absurdity. "But one nonetheless."

"We are here to encourage your engagement to continue," Worthington answered.

Ravencroft bit out a harsh laugh. "What a diplomatic approach."

They were at a standstill. Ravencroft wanted them to make a demand either way, but they refused, which left him to state his intentions. Did he wish to continue with the engagement? Or did he want to withdraw his offer and disappear back to his estate? He stared at the gentlemen across from him as they waited for his answer. The easygoing brother sat with patience, while the older brother stewed in his chair, demanding an answer with this steely gaze.

Ravencroft leapt to his feet and started pacing around the room. They assumed they had him trapped without options. With each pass around the study, he realized he held no other choice. It didn't help that a lingering scent of lilacs hovered near his desk. He paused and placed his hand on the desk, closing his eyes as he considered his response.

A tempting angel invaded his thoughts. Her warm lips opened against his onslaught of kisses that his sinful demands echoed. Her reaction to his scandalous words strummed through him. He opened his eyes and spun toward the door. His steps took him outside, and everything from the night before came flashing back.

Noel had come to make her own demands. Her visit no more differed from her brothers. In his resistance, he had struck at her with demanding kisses and assaulted her senses with his vulgarity. He had done so to frighten her away. Instead, he had awakened her desires.

His gaze swept the garden as he detailed her every move. They had moved inside where he propositioned her on how she could satisfy his urges. He remembered the heat in her gaze. She might have fled in shock, but her body responded to him with untamed passion.

A wicked smile spread across his lips once he reached his decision. He would give Noel's brothers an answer to appease them, one he would find tremendous in pleasure once he achieved the outcome of his desires.

His steps drew him back inside with a bland expression. "With your permission, I would like to continue our engagement. I look forward to my marriage to Noel."

Ravencroft appeared the humble servant to the Worthington gentlemen. He held the ability to project himself and gain the acceptance of his worth from his peers. However, he already planned how to woo Noel and gain Lady Worthington's forgiveness for his absence. The Worthingtons were under the impression they held the power to control him, but it was the complete opposite.

Worthington narrowed his gaze and observed Ravencroft with a shrewdness most men would cower from. However, Ravencroft stood tall with confidence. After a while, Worthington nodded his acceptance. Then he stood and left without issuing a reply.

Worth stepped forward and held out his hand. "Thank you."

Ravencroft held in his snide smile and instead offered a polite one of indifference. "My pleasure."

Worth cleared his throat. "Mother wanted us to issue an invitation to dinner this evening."

"You may tell her of my acceptance."

Worth nodded. "Good day."

Ravencroft waited until the front door closed before he released a wicked chuckle, the very same one he had released when Noel fled. Perhaps he was too harsh with his mother. After all, if he had never deceived the Worthingtons, then he never would have discovered the passion Noel kept suppressed, a passion he eagerly waited to explore. And to think he thought her an angel.

When in fact she was sin's very own temptation.

Chapter Four

NOEL FOUGHT THROUGH THE drowsiness, only to fall back into darkness again. She lost count of how many times this occurred. When she finally awakened, she realized whoever kept her captive also continued drugging her. Her body shivered on the cot.

The first time she had awakened, they had tied her hands behind her back. However, they had since freed one of her hands and secured the other one to the cot. She saw a cup on the stand next to her, and her dry mouth begged for a drink. However, she feared it was the source of what kept her drugged.

When keys rattled at the door, she closed her eyes and relaxed her body, pretending to sleep. She had practiced this technique when she was younger to avoid her parents when they fought. The shuffling of feet near the cot drew her attention. She didn't dare open her eyes to see who they belonged to, but she must prepare herself before the kidnappers confronted her.

"Lady L will not appreciate you feeding her," the young girl hissed.

"But I cannot have the girl thinking ill thoughts of me," an older lady cooed.

"You are hopeless."

The older lady tsked. "Jealousy will get you nowhere, my dear."

The young girl blew out a breath. "What is there to be jealous of?"

The older lady appeared to console the younger girl. "I understand how heart-wrenching it is to see how Dracott has found someone else to love."

The younger girl never offered a reply, but Noel sensed her unhappiness. Who was this girl to Dracott and did he love her? If so, why did he profess to love Maggie and want to marry her? Was this another ploy in their deception with Lady Langdale? Noel needed answers and hoped to learn more. The more leverage she had against them, the more it would aid in her escape.

The young girl laughed. "So where did your brutes find her?"

"Outside of the Worthington townhome. However, I am confused as to why she donned her britches. It must be some game of theirs. I will never understand my youngest child."

The young girl only found amusement in the older lady's explanation. "I cannot wait for Lady L to see your surprise."

Noel couldn't stand it any longer, not after the lady declared herself Dracott's mother. The lady was also Ravencroft's mother, and she didn't realize she had grabbed the wrong Worthington daughter. However, the other girl realized Lady Ravencroft's mistake and took pleasure from it.

Noel opened her eyes into the slightest of slits and watched the younger girl make herself comfortable on the chair against the wall, while the older lady preened in front of the mirror.

After wiping away a smidge of lip color from her mouth and patting her hair into place, the older lady turned toward Noel. She tilted her head to the side, and her lips twisted in her perusal before she walked closer to the cot. Noel lowered her eyes and deepened her breathing.

"She looks older than I thought she was. The Worthington ladies must not age well," Lady Ravencroft stated.

Her observation brought forth another bout of laughter from the other girl. Noel fought to keep her face still when she actually wanted to pinch her lips together in displeasure. How dare she insult the ladies in Noel's family? She was a horrid woman.

"You still don't see your mistake, do you?" the younger girl asked.

"And what mistake might that be?"

"I too am curious about what mistake Lady Ravencroft has made." Another voice spoke from the doorway. "More importantly, what do we have here?"

Lady Ravencroft beamed with pride over her surprise. "My men have brought you Dracott's bride."

"Mmm, have they?"

Noel listened to the new arrival murmur who she guessed to be the infamous Lady Langdale. After one glance, the lady knew who Noel was. However, Ravencroft's mother still hadn't realized her mistake. She kept twittering along about how they had captured her.

"She was just standing outside their gate."

"And you found nothing strange about her dressed as a boy on her wedding night, outside alone?" Lady L asked.

Lady Ravencroft's hands fluttered in the air. "I figured it was some game she played with Dracott." She nodded over at the other girl. "You know how his tastes run."

Noel heard a chair clatter to the floor and a shriek. Her eyes flew open to witness the young girl advancing on Lady Ravencroft with her arm pulled back and her hand tightened into a fist. Lady Ravencroft cowered in the corner with her hands pulled over her face. However, before the girl took another step, she dropped her hand and shook her head in disgust. Then she turned to leave.

"Stop," Lady L demanded. "Were you a part of this?"

The girl scoffed. "No. I only wanted to watch once she realized the error of her goons."

"Yes. She has made a grave error. But I am sure our guest will understand that it was nothing personal." Lady L turned to face Noel. "Won't you, my dear?"

Noel refused to answer. Instead, she sat up to the best of her ability and tilted her chin as if they were subjects below her regard, which only drew laughter from Lady L and the young girl.

"Yes. She is most definitely a Worthington and shares the same haughty attitude as her brother. Even though she is the wrong sister, she will do," Lady L commented.

Lady Ravencroft's face pinched in confusion. "But I brought you the one who wears breeches. This is Maggie."

"I have no clue why the lady dressed as she has. But she is not Maggie Worthington. Maggie and Dracott are at Mivart's, enjoying their wedding stay," Lady L disagreed.

"Then she must be a servant. I will have the men get rid of her body." Lady Ravencroft wiped her hands together.

Lady L sighed with exasperation. "Did you not hear what I said? She is not a mere servant but one of Worthington's sisters. She will do nicely. For my sake anyway. Unfortunately for you, not so much."

The young girl chuckled. "She still does not realize who she has captured. One must laugh at the absurdity of the situation, even as despicable as it may be."

"That is enough. I will take care of Lady Ravencroft's mistake. You are to change your clothes. I have laid out a dress for you to wear for this evening's entertainment." She pointed at the door for the girl to leave.

"I am not playing dress-up." The girl stomped her foot.

"Yes, you will. A little birdie told me this afternoon about how one of my marks has become enamored with you. He saw you at the theatre and has searched for you relentlessly. However, he has found no luck with finding you. Your job this evening is to give him another peek and lead him astray. You are the perfect distraction for him." Lady L's devious smile matched the vindictiveness in her eyes.

The girl glanced at Noel with unease but looked away quickly. Why did the girl hold guilt over Lady L's order? Who was the gentleman interested in her? Did it make the girl uncomfortable? Why did her look hold desperation? Why was this girl involved with Lady L's gang? Instead of gaining answers to her dilemma, she only had more questions that plagued her.

"Now!" Lady L hissed.

The young girl growled her frustration. Noel expected her to throw a tantrum, but she didn't. Instead, she walked out the door, throwing over her shoulder, "Welcome to our humble home, Lady Noel Worthington."

Lady Ravencroft gasped at the astonishing reveal as the girl's laughter echoed behind her. Noel's gaze shifted to Ravencroft's mother to watch her eyes widen and her face turn pale. Lady Ravencroft's gaze flew back and forth between Lady L and Noel as the impact of her mistake hit her. The consequences she faced would be insurmountable.

"No. No. No," Lady Ravencroft cried, shaking her head back and forth.

"I am afraid so. She will work nicely with my plans, but I fear she will ruin your plans to reenter society. I do not think Ravencroft will take kindly to his mother kidnapping his fiancée." Lady L made a tsking noise.

Noel remained silent. Neither lady required her to talk, and she had nothing to say. It was not as if she had any leverage to demand her release. She would remain calm and wait for reinforcements. Before long, her family would discover her absence and begin their search. With the recent threats from Lady L, they would realize who was behind Noel's disappearance.

"What if we let her go? She can explain to her family how she made her escape when her kidnappers left her unattended and how they never showed their faces to her," Lady Ravencroft suggested.

With each comment from this lady, Noel found it difficult to remain stoic. She couldn't believe this was Ravencroft's mother and hoped he didn't carry any of her traits. She had learned the evening before that her fiancé wasn't who he had portrayed himself to be all these months. He had given a false impression of a gentleman when he was really a scoundrel with nefarious traits. The lady before her displayed her selfishness by only thinking of herself. Perhaps this was all a trick. She couldn't be his mother. Because even with his scandalous behavior last night, Ravencroft's primary objective was to protect her. This lady only protected herself. Also, she was Dracott's mother, and from the time she spent in his company, Dracott had only displayed honorable intentions.

"If we release her, she will inform her brothers who held her. Also, Ravencroft will learn it was you who kidnapped her. My men didn't steal her away, yours did. No. Unfortunately, we must keep her until I finish my special mission. When we leave London, we will return Lady Noel to her family. In the meantime, I shall have her moved into your quarters." Lady L looked around the room in disgust. "This place is not suitable for a guest of Lady Noel's esteem."

"You cannot. Where will I sleep?" Lady Ravencroft protested.

Lady L spread her hands out. "Why, here, Lady Ravencroft. After all, it was your fault, so you must bear the unfortunate circumstances of your mistake." Lady L moved to Noel and untied her restraint. "Come, Lady Noel. I will show you to more pleasant accommodations."

Noel didn't understand what to make of the dynamics before her. Lady Ravencroft stood in a bumbling mess with tears streaming down her face. What Noel found most strange was how she never argued with Lady L on her absurd notion.

Noel followed slowly, taking in every detail along the way. She wasn't a fool. Lady L might move her into a more comfortable bedchamber, but the same treatment would befall her. They wouldn't allow her free rein over the house. They would sequester her in a room, making her a prisoner until they achieved the level of chaos intended for her family and the ton.

Lady L swept into a room filled with frilly lace everywhere, from the pillowcases to the curtains hanging from the windows. When Noel stepped close to them, Lady L shook her head and shooed her away. "I am sorry, *my lady*. But you must stay clear from the windows."

Noel cringed at the emphasis Lady Langdale placed on her status, but she obeyed for the moment and sat on a chair by the fireplace. She folded her hands in her lap and waited for the lady to proceed. Lady L had much to say, and she was more than eager to listen. Noel had made a mistake by not listening to Dracott's story, but she wouldn't make the same mistake twice.

Lady L sat across from Noel. "You are rather quiet. Are you not feeling your usual self? I only ask because from what I have observed, you are quite the chatterbox. Tittering on about this or that to anyone who would listen. You are not what I expected Ravencroft to settle with."

Noel arched an eyebrow. Lady L's comment held just the right innuendo for Noel to speak. "Why ever not? What type of lady did you imagine him settling with?"

Lady L pretended interest in her nails, but Noel noticed her smirk. "Someone with a little more flair. And passion. Someone whose fire kept him on his toes and chasing after her. No offense, my dear. You seem a little tame for a man whose passion runs deep. But then again, that is why men have mistresses. Who wants fire and passion in a marriage bed when you can have it with someone you owe no obligation to? It is less messy that way."

Noel gulped. Lady L appeared confident about what Ravencroft needed. Before last night, Noel would have argued that Lady L was mistaken. However, Ravencroft's behavior showed the truth of Lady L's statement. "And how exactly are you aware of what Ravencroft requires?"

Lady L gave Noel a sympathetic smile before rising. "I will have a tray delivered to you. Please stay in your room. I have positioned my guards around the house, so an escape is impossible. For your safety, I must warn you not to attempt one. If you do, then I fear the harm that may befall you. Enjoy your stay, my lady."

Lady L glided out of the room, closing the door softly behind her. She left without answering Noel's question, which left Noel to wonder how intimate Ravencroft had been with Lady L and if they still were.

Noel had never imagined when she snuck away how awakened she would become.

Chapter Five

RAVENCROFT WALKED TO THE Worthington townhome along the back lane, savoring the smokey flavor of his cigar. Noel detested them, and he hoped that, by smoking one, it would keep her at a distance. His conscience had bothered him throughout the day on his behavior the evening before and his decision to pursue her with scandalous intentions. His conflicted thoughts had led him to write Noel a letter. A damn love letter at that. However, he had come to his senses before he sent it to her.

He refused to surrender now and must stand by the decision he made. His tantalizing thoughts of Noel spread out on his bed while he built her desires to the heights of ecstasy fueled his determination. He had underestimated her when he chose her for a bride. She wasn't meek or mild by any standards. She was a fiery goddess who set his soul on fire. And he wanted to make her burn as he did.

Ravencroft leaned against the gate while he finished smoking. It would appear to most that he stalled before facing the Worthingtons. However, he only wanted to annoy them a bit with his insolence. Reese Worthington threw his power around and expected his family to obey his rules. At first, he had followed along so society would accept him back into their fold. However, he no longer cared if the patriarch cared for him or not since he had achieved what he set out to do.

They were in no position to deny him. If they did, then Noel would become a pariah, and just after their family regained their stellar reputation amongst the ton. The elder Worthington had made quite a reputation for himself as a degenerate louse who ran with a raucous crowd, one that included Ravencroft's mother. His death had brought shame upon the family, along with empty purse strings. Very similar to Ravencroft's own circumstances. However, Worthington had made a match with the Duke of Colebourne's niece and found himself sitting quite nicely. Ravencroft was under the opinion it wouldn't hurt the earl to repay in kind.

"One would think you are trying to irritate my brother with your delay," Worth quipped.

Ravencroft smiled. He didn't mind the younger brother. In fact, he quite enjoyed the time he spent playing cards or riding horses with Worth. The difference between the brothers shouldn't surprise him. Hell, he and Dracott were as different as two brothers could be.

He dropped the cigar and smashed it with his boot. "Is it working?"

Worth slapped him on the back. "Yes. I applaud your achievement. Between you and Noel, he has worked himself into a frenzy today."

Ravencroft frowned. "What has Noel done?"

Worth shrugged. "She has holed herself up in her bedchamber."

"With the danger surrounding your family, none of you find that strange?"

"There are men guarding the house," Worth explained.

"What makes you think she hasn't snuck away?" Ravencroft asked.

"It is typical Noel fashion. She is upset Maggie married before her. Mama says to allow Noel her privacy, and she will return to her old self after your visit."

Ravencroft nodded. However, Worth's explanation didn't settle his mind. It wasn't like Noel to pout like a petulant child. But then again, after her visit, he had learned what a walking contradiction she was.

"Where are you off to?" Ravencroft asked.

Worth's seriousness disappeared, and a grin lit his face. "I have it on excellent authority that a lady who I have taken an interest in will be at a private dinner party I plan to crash."

Ravencroft chuckled. "Well, at least one of us will enjoy ourselves this evening."

Worth nodded. "Good luck."

"I will need it." Ravencroft strolled through the garden to the open doors of the drawing room.

The ladies sat waiting for dinner while Worthington paced back and forth. He glared when Ravencroft entered, then focused his attention back on the hallway. The earl would make his return difficult. At least the ladies seem pleased with his appearance.

Lady Worthington rose. "How lovely of you to join us this evening, Gregory."

He bowed. "It is my pleasure. On my way in, I spoke with Worth. He mentioned Lady Noel was not feeling well. I hope you can persuade her to enjoy dinner with us."

"If not, I will drag her down myself," Worthington growled.

Evelyn glided over to her husband and whispered to him, coaxing a smile to his lips. After a few more words, she turned toward them. "I will check on her. Mama, please inform Rogers there will be a slight delay in dinner."

"All right, dear. Also, please tell Noel that Gregory has arrived." Lady Worthington smiled over at him.

Ravencroft inwardly sighed in relief. From all standards, everyone appeared accepting of his return. Except for Worthington, whose glare stated he still held onto his disapproval. Did Noel hold the same feelings as her brother? Why else would she remain in her bedchamber?

An awkward silence settled over the room as they waited for Evelyn and Noel to join them. Ravencroft didn't want to discuss the wedding since he hadn't shown his support for his brother's union to Maggie. In his misery, he had drunk his shame away after the Worthingtons learned of their secrets. However, it still lingered, clinging to him in dishonor. He was ashamed of his behavior and his dishonesty.

Eden offered him an encouraging smile, and he attempted one in return. However, the longer the silence stretched, the more he worried something was wrong with Noel. Was Evelyn having difficulty persuading Noel to come downstairs? If so, he would take his leave and attempt a visit tomorrow.

"Perhaps if I call tomorrow, Noel will join you for dinner," Ravencroft suggested.

"No. She must learn that one cannot run from their problems because it solves nothing. It only makes them more difficult to deal with," Worthington disagreed.

"I will see what is taking so long," Eden offered.

Before Eden left, Evelyn came rushing into the drawing room. The stricken expression on her face confirmed Ravencroft's suspicions.

"She is not here," he declared.

Evelyn shook her head. "No, she is not."

"How do you know that? What have you done with her?" Worthington accused.

"I wish I had her. Then I would've kept her safe and out of harm's way," Ravencroft growled.

Worthington and Ravencroft advanced on each other. Neither of them trusted the other.

Before any fists could fly, Eden stepped in between them. "Stop! Fighting amongst ourselves will not bring Noel home safely."

"Where are they keeping her?" Worthington accused again.

Ravencroft gritted his teeth, fighting back his denial in Noel's disappearance. However, it was his fault she had gone missing. If he had discarded his pride after Dracott confessed, then Noel never would have left the safety of her home. Now she was at the mercy of a lady whose only agenda was revenge. He should've followed her immediately and watched her enter the townhome. Instead, he had waited too long, and when he didn't see Noel, he had assumed she had already returned inside.

He turned his back on the Worthington family, running his hands through his hair in frustration. He thought by refusing to help either party, he could avoid his involvement in capturing Lady L or falling victim to his mother's schemes. But it appeared it was now out of his hands. He would need to join Lady L's forces to secure Noel's release.

"Lord Worthington?" Rogers interrupted from the doorway.

"We are not ready to dine yet," Evelyn said before Reese unleashed his fury on the servant.

Rogers cleared his throat. "I understand. However, someone has delivered a note, and I thought it urgent to bring it in."

Worthington held out his hand. "Does someone await a reply?"

Rogers shook his head. "No. He scampered away before he even handed the letter over."

"Damn. We cannot follow him," Eden muttered.

"Eden Worthington!" Lady Worthington reprimanded.

"My apologies, Mama, for uttering my frustration."

Ravencroft would've laughed at the proper decorum if he wasn't worried over Noel's welfare. He held no clue about Lady L's state of mind. With each second Noel remained under her capture, she risked becoming a victim to Lady Langdale's cruelty. And Barbara Langdale enjoyed nothing more than terrorizing someone above her in rank.

"Hand me the letter," Worthington ordered.

Ravencroft turned and saw the butler's discomfort. He had learned from Dracott how Worthington kept Rogers employed to watch him after they revealed Rogers's connection to Dracott. He sympathized with the man because it was why Worthington forced him to stay engaged to Noel. Worthington went by the old saying of keeping your enemies close. While neither man was a threat, they held a past connection to the villain who tormented his family.

"The letter is for Lord Ravencroft." Rogers walked over to him and handed over the letter before Worthington took possession of it.

Ravencroft peered in confusion at the folded parchment. Then he noticed his mother's handwriting and ripped it open. However, it wasn't his mother who penned the missive but Lady L herself. She teased him before making her demand.

Lord Ravencroft,

Your mother gifted me today with a present I threatened to take if you didn't assist me in my latest caper. Much to my surprise, she thought I would enjoy it, not realizing the impact it would have on her relationship with you. But who is it for me to turn down such a generous offering?

I must say, after spending a few moments alone with the chit, I am quite surprised at your choice for a bride. Oh, I understand all that nonsense of coin and status you will gain with your marriage to a Worthington. I am sure Reese will be most generous with his sister's dowry. He always was as a lover. But Gregory darling, she has no spirit. She sits all haughty, like she is above me. No passion. No fight. My dear, I fear you will endure a dull marriage. But then, as I informed your fiancée, that is what mistresses are for. Something I have much experience with. In which case I might have elaborated with details to Lady Noel.

Now for what I require of you. Well, you already know. I do not think I need to repeat my request now that I hold the bargaining chip in our negotiations. I expect I will hear from you soon.

Oh, and please send Reese my love. I miss our decadent nights together.

Yours truly,

Barbara

Ravencroft snarled his displeasure, gripping the letter. He couldn't even direct his anger at the lady who wrote it. No. She only used the opportunity to her advantage. His own mother worked against him. Did the woman not hold an ounce of decency in her soul? Why did he even assume she might? His entire life, he had watched how she acted for her benefit alone and not for those she professed to love. Why should his future happiness with Noel be any different? His mother saw this as an opportunity to fall back into Lady L's good graces since she had failed to convince him and Dracott to return to the chaos. They forced his hand, leaving him with no other option than to betray the Worthingtons.

"Where can I find her?" Ravencroft asked Rogers.

"Give me the letter," Worthington demanded.

Ravencroft thrust the note into his pocket. "No."

"I have every right to read it. She is my sister and no longer your fiancée," Worthington threatened.

Ravencroft's bitter laughter caused everyone in the room discomfort. He no longer cared. His only objective was to rescue Noel. The rest of them could hold whatever opinion they wanted of him. After he rescued her, he would leave London and never return. He thought he wanted to return to this life, but he was mistaken. Now he understood why his father sequestered himself at their estate, content to live a simple life.

"Out of respect for your wife, I will keep the letter to myself." He arched a brow to relay implications in the letter pertaining to Reese's affair with Barbara Langdale.

His comment drew the ladies' attention away from him to Worthington. They ranged from disgust to disappointment and despair.

He strode to Rogers's side. "Where is she?"

"I do not know, my lord," Rogers denied.

"You must. How else did you help Ren?" Ravencroft asked.

"She found me," Rogers whispered.

"Who is Ren?" Eden asked from behind them.

Ravencroft stilled. As much as he didn't care for Dracott's little friend, he wouldn't expose her identity to the Worthingtons. She was still under Lady L's guard and had more to risk than anyone else.

"You misunderstand me, Lady Eden. I asked Rogers *when* did he last see Lady Langdale." Ravencroft turned on his charming smile.

Eden narrowed her gaze, refusing to fall for his false charm. After learning of his duplicity in character, she understood why Maggie always thought he acted false. It would appear there were many sides to Lord Ravencroft, and it was best that Reese withdrew his support for Noel to marry Ravencroft. Eden no longer trusted him, but she would play along to discover his secrets.

She wasn't the only Worthington who held the skill of pretending she was somebody she wasn't. She had perfected her acting skills while working alongside Worth and Ralston. They had taught her how everyone limited their perception to how you presented yourself and looked no deeper because the drama surrounding them captivated their attention. Ravencroft was no different.

Even now, Ravencroft played them false. He appeared concerned for Noel's welfare, when in fact he only held concern for himself. He held his secrets close, revealing nothing unless he needed to. Eden decided right then that her mission was to keep a close eye on Ravencroft while they secured Noel's rescue. He would reveal his hand soon enough.

"I apologize. I misheard what you said. Ren? When? They sound so similar." She returned his smile with her own charming one.

Eden didn't fool Ravencroft in the slightest with her flighty act. Hell, he admired her for it. She didn't realize it, but she would be a formable asset in her sister's rescue, and he would use her skills when needed. Except now, he must search for Lady L and didn't have the slightest idea where to start. He had hoped Rogers had information about her hideout, but Rogers spoke the truth.

"Excuse me, sir, but a young lad has arrived, asking for you. He waits in the kitchen," a footman stuttered to Rogers, wearing a look of sheer panic for interrupting them.

Rogers smiled with the patience of a butler, calming another servant. But Ravencroft didn't miss the slight astonishment on Rogers's face at the news the servant delivered. "I will be along shortly. Please settle the lad in my office." At the footman's nod, Rogers turned back to Ravencroft and Eden. "If you will excuse me, I must see to this matter."

"Of course, Rogers." Eden walked back over to her family, who were discussing Noel's disappearance. She noticed how Rogers and Ravencroft tensed at the footman's news. However, nothing appeared out of the ordinary at the disturbance. It must be her imagination since she didn't trust Ravencroft.

Ravencroft exchanged a glance with Rogers to keep his disturbance in his office for as long as he could. "They have Noel," he whispered before speaking louder. "Thank you for your help, Rogers."

He turned back to the Worthington family. Evelyn sat comforting Lady Worthington, while Eden and Reese whispered amongst each other, most likely about her suspicions of him. No matter how it would appear, he must leave now. Ren would run as soon as she informed Rogers of Noel's abduction. She came to deliver the news because of her loyalty to Dracott. She wouldn't stay around for Ravencroft to interrogate her. Each second he remained as a concerned fiancé with Noel's family, it was a second he lost in finding her.

He strode toward the doors leading to the garden. He would leave the way he came and circle around to the servant's entrance. Once Ren left, he would follow her to Noel.

However, Worthington wouldn't make it easy for him to escape.

Worthington swung him around. "Where are you going? We need to find Noel."

Ravencroft brushed off his hold. "I am off to find Worth. He told me of his plans for the evening, and I thought he would help us organize a search party."

Lady Worthington sniffed. "A wonderful suggestion, Ravencroft. I can see why Noel loves you as she does. Your calmness during a crisis is an admirable trait."

He retraced his steps and knelt to her level, gathering her hands in his. "I promise I will help bring Noel back to you."

Lady Worthington squeezed his hands. "I have faith you will."

Her faith in him humbled Ravencroft. The lady before him held the traits of how a mother should care for her children. Her generosity and ability to forgive made him want to prove how worthy he was for Noel. While everyone else doubted him, this woman gave her trust to him with an open heart, just as her daughter had. He may have his own nefarious reasons for finding Noel, but it didn't lessen this woman's faith any.

Before anyone questioned his motives, he left. He only hoped he didn't miss his one opportunity to find where they hid Noel. Ravencroft rushed around to the servant's entrance to see Ren running from the townhome. Rogers followed her, calling out her name in desperation to keep her there. But the sprite kept running. When Rogers spotted Ravencroft, he stopped and bent over to catch his breath. Ravencroft took off after her and stayed close enough so she would notice him. She looked over her shoulder and slowed down once she saw Rogers no longer followed her.

Ren turned the corner, and Ravencroft continued after her. However, when he reached the road, he found it empty. Damn. He'd lost her. He pounded his fist on the building he leaned against. Where did she go? Ren held the ability to lose anyone who followed her. Dracott had taught her how to stay aware of her surroundings and how to protect herself from danger. In his current state of frustration, Ravencroft was a danger Ren didn't want to find herself tangled with.

Taunting laughter stirred the air. Ravencroft tensed, standing to attention. The laughter wasn't a threat, but more of a taunt at his inadequate skill to best her.

"Where is she keeping her?"

She reversed his question on him. "Where is who keeping whom?"

Ravencroft fought to remain calm. It was always a battle of will between them, and he wouldn't allow his frustration to bring about her victory. He needed to change tactics and focus on her vulnerability. "I am sorry for your loss."

"Loss? It is not I who has lost anything but you."

He didn't reply to her taunt and continued with his. "It must be heartbreaking to see how he loves another so profoundly."

"You never understood our friendship," she hissed.

"Friendship? Mmm. Is that what you called it? And I thought you each cared more deeply than a simple friendship," Ravencroft baited her.

Her silence meant that his comment unsettled her. He hadn't watched their infatuation for years to misunderstand the connection. Hell. Dracott had secured the girl's freedom with a promise to return to her. If their connection wasn't because of love, what was it then? No. The chit hiding in the shadows must be heartbroken over his brother's marriage to Maggie Worthington. Why else would she lead him on this merry chase without seeking her own revenge over having knowledge of Noel's whereabouts?

Ravencroft attempted to persuade her to help him. "Ren, there is no need to make this difficult. Just lead me to Lady L's hideout. I will wait for you to make yourself scarce before presenting myself."

Only the silence continued. Ren had disappeared. He had pushed her too far, and he was still no closer to discovering Noel's whereabouts. Once again, his jealousy over Dracott and

Ren's connection was his downfall. He leaned his head against the building and blew out a pent-up breath he didn't realize he held. When would he ever learn?

Ravencroft walked back to the Worthingtons' townhome. Since Rogers didn't wait outside for his return, it meant he didn't have any news to relay. Ren's appearance was only to warn Rogers that Lady L held Noel prisoner so he could inform Dracott. He continued to his townhome to think of a plan. It was useless to find Worth because he held no clue where the gentleman had taken himself off to. He had only lied to the Worthingtons to make his own escape. It seemed he was only capable of deception.

Lies upon lies. They were the very reason he found himself in his current predicament.

Chapter Six

NOEL SIGHED AGAIN AS she wandered around the small bedchamber. While it was clean, it held a sense of proclivity to sin that made her uncomfortable. In her boredom, she peeked inside the wardrobe and found many indecent garments. The lace displayed throughout the bedchamber gave the impression that a proper lady resided within, but her clothing showed proof of the lady's sinfulness.

Two men had entered the bedchamber and boarded the windows after Lady L left. She took their presence more of Lady Langdale reiterating her threat not to attempt an escape. Noel feared for her safety by the sheer size of the guards. It wouldn't take much for them to break her in two. And the scowls they'd delivered her way confirmed their dislike of her presence. While Noel dealt with ladies similar to Lady L's and Lady Ravencroft's character since her debut a few years ago, she had been fortunate enough to never acquaint herself with men of this class. Were they men or forces of nature meant only to deliver harm?

Each time she attempted to open the door, she found it locked. While the guards scared her, she wondered if they only relied on their strength to enforce Lady L's orders. Or could she outsmart them with her wit alone? However, she never got the chance because after they delivered her meals, they locked the door behind them.

Which left Noel to wonder over her fate. Not only her fate but her relationship with Ravencroft. It made her question the false security she held in their engagement. Maybe she was the dim-witted debutante everyone thought she was. How else could she have mistaken Ravencroft's character? His disreputable behavior when he kissed her displayed a rake whose only intention was to bed her.

The memories washed over her with a determination to understand the shift in their relationship. Her body grew warm, as if Ravencroft were present, and a need consumed her that she didn't understand. What would've happened if she hadn't run away and instead indulged in every indecent suggestion Ravencroft made? Would she find pleasure in the sinful suggestions Ravencroft enticed her with?

Her body trembled as she envisioned them wrapped in each other's embrace. Her hand slid along her chest, brushing across her nipples. They tightened under the shirt and ached from her slightest touch. She slid her fingers across them again to help ease the ache. However, it only caused her body to stir with desire. Her wicked thoughts led her on an unfamiliar path.

How would it feel for Ravencroft to nestle his head between her breasts and suckle on her nipples for hours on end? Would his passion be gentle? Or would he dominate her senses with his demanding mouth? Noel's body tingled with each thought.

She jumped from the chair and slammed the door to the wardrobe. This bedchamber drew out her forbidden thoughts and taunted her with what she might never experience. That thought alone prompted her to open the wardrobe and stroke her hand along a silken negligee. The bold color of red tempted her with a night filled with scandalous interludes.

Images flooded her senses of lying spread out on Ravencroft's desk as he whispered into her ear, seducing her into succumbing to his wildest fantasies. Did Ravencroft find Noel attractive in a sexual nature? Or did his taste run more to the Lady Langdales of the world? She drew the negligee out and held it to her body. She shifted to the mirror to look at herself. The red complimented her golden tresses, turning them into a warm shade of sunshine. Her fingers sank into the softness of the silk. Would it caress her skin the way Ravencroft had?

Noel glanced over her shoulder at the door and wondered if she should dare. The house had grown quiet after they served her dinner, and she didn't think anyone would bother her this evening. Her teeth dug into her bottom lip and gnawed back and forth while she worked up her nerve to try the scandalous garment on. The longer she debated with herself, the more the thrill of draping herself in the wanton gown enticed her to step behind the dressing screen and tug off her clothes.

She shivered in the cool air as it washed over her nakedness. The act of standing without a stitch of clothing on in a strange home shocked Noel, and she refused to ponder the feelings it ignited. She donned the gown, and it slid over her body with a gentleness only a generous lover would offer. After she took a step forward, Noel gasped at her revealed leg. She moved her leg back to see it once again covered, only to move again with an urgency to see how the negligee flowed around her. It was like nothing she had ever worn before.

She scampered to the mirror in her eagerness and stood in shock at the beauty before her. Her hand stretched out to touch the glass, her fingers trailing a path at every indecent part of herself revealed. As her fingers explored her exposed skin, she felt a singe in the valley between her breasts. When she shifted her hand from the mirror to herself, she gasped at the intimacy of her own caress. Her nipples budded out against the material, revealing themselves with enough to tease a gentleman into having explicit thoughts.

Noel twirled slowly in a circle, loving how the bold gown clung to her curves. Her hands shimmied along the silk, heightening her fascination with how such a thin scrap of fabric gave one the confidence to pursue their desires. To make one bold enough to tempt the gentleman of her dreams to indulge in a night of sin. Would Ravencroft slack his desires if she were to wear this for him?

She floated around the bedchamber as if she and Ravencroft shared a dance of temptation. She watched how her leg teased itself from the slit in the gown with each twirl she took. After blowing out the candles, she settled on the lace-covered mattress. There was no light to offer her any comfort, just eerie blackness. Her body shuddered as she listened to the house creak with its every movement.

Noel closed her eyes, remembering the comfort of Ravencroft's kisses. They held no gentleness a lady might feel from her first kiss. The kisses were as bold as the gown she wore with each mind-consuming pull of his lips against hers. They dominated her senses with the power he kept clenched, refusing to combust and drown her with his desire. Her thoughts kept leaping with curiosity about how Ravencroft would act if he unleashed the passion on her soul.

Noel lost herself in her fantasy as it changed to a dream and sleep drew her within its grasp. Her last thought was if Ravencroft would find her desirable in the sinfully red negligee.

However, it never mattered because, in her dream, he did.

Ravencroft spent most of the evening pacing in his study, his mind consumed with how to find Noel. Each time he passed his desk, images of her spread out before him clouded his thoughts. He should keep his attention focused on how he would return Noel to her family, but he was powerless in his sinful fantasies. If he found her, would he return her to the bosom of her home? Or would he kidnap her for himself and ravish her senseless? Strip her bare and feast on her delights. He felt unbalanced, like a caged animal. He hadn't experienced this desperation since his mother forced him into a life of crime. Once he escaped that life, he had refused to enter it again. Also, he refused to become a victim of his emotions.

After savoring Noel's lips once, he had fallen victim to the instability of becoming vulnerable to another soul. While he cared for his brother, he had always kept their relationship separate from his heart. Now he risked exposing his heart to a lady who deserved more than he could offer her. However, he was a greedy bastard who would seduce her until she fell victim to the hell of his existence.

His hands shook, wanting to reach for the bottle of whiskey his maid had replaced in the study, but he refrained. Losing himself in spirits wouldn't help Noel's cause. No, he must keep his wits about him until they summoned him. Which should be anytime now. He knew how Lady L played tricks with one's mind. She dangled the letter at him, full of clues about how she would reveal her hiding spot once she saw fit to.

It was why he had returned to his home instead of the Worthingtons. He needed to make himself available or lose the chance to rescue Noel. Also, it was best he stayed away from Worthington for the sake of their family. He no longer had to tolerate the earl's authority. He would stand as his own man and to hell with whoever didn't approve.

"My lady, you cannot go in there," Ravencroft heard the maid ordering someone in the hallway.

The maid rushed in after the lady, pulling at her arm to stop her from entering. The scene would have been most comical if Noel's safety wasn't a worry for him. A simple maid attempted to prevent his mother from entering a place she used to call home. However, the maid held no clue who the lady was. He must interrupt them before his mother threatened the poor girl's life. His financial standing kept him from employing quality servants. He hated to lose the ones he had acquired.

"That will be all, Meg. I can handle it from here," Ravencroft assured the maid.

Meg curtsied, a blush spreading across her cheeks at being called her by her name. "Very well, my lord."

His mother arched her eyebrow at the exchange. He rolled his eyes at her unspoken comment. He thought she would keep her opinion to herself on the matter, but then he should've known better.

"I see they still fall at your feet at every opportunity. She is a pretty chit. Does she warm your bedsheets at night as well as serve you throughout the day? If so, it must be a strenuous position she holds. I hope you pay her well." Lady Ravencroft peeled off her gloves and swiped her finger along the bookcase. "At least she is skilled with a feather duster."

Once he crossed paths with his mother after his father passed away, he had learned how best it was to stay silent with her vulgar opinions. To comment would only provoke her into demeaning her subject. He would hate for Meg or the other servants to overhear his mother. Nor did he want them to learn this lady was his mother. He preferred to keep this information to himself.

Ravencroft strode to the door to close it. His servants would eavesdrop, and he needed to keep the conversation filtered the best he could. "Is there a reason for your call?"

Lady Ravencroft fluttered her fingers in the air. "Are you not going to offer me some refreshments?"

He crossed his arms over his chest and leaned against the door. "I see no reason for this to become a social call."

Her nose twitched in distaste at the state of his furniture before she settled in a chair. "But I come bearing news."

"Of course you have. So let's hear it, so you can be on your way and I can settle the matter that needs attending."

Lady Ravencroft huffed. "This is not how you should treat your *mother*."

Ravencroft cringed at the pitch in her tone. She was staking her claim to his parentage to whoever might listen. "Enough," he snarled. "Lay out the terms."

Lady Ravencroft's appearance took on a pinched expression at his tone. Her attempt at stalling her confession of kidnapping the wrong Worthington sister wasn't falling into her plans. She tried not to cringe at the anger she would invoke once she admitted her mishap. Even though she held a perfect explanation for her guards' confusion, Ravencroft wouldn't see it in that manner. While she had never noticed him holding tender regard for the girl, he was protective of the girl's feelings. He doted on her, fooling everyone who didn't know his true character. However, she knew when her son played someone false. And Noel Worthington was his latest victim.

She smoothed her hand along her skirt, wiping away the dampness. Her son was the complete opposite of his father. Her late husband had been gentle and kind and catered to her every whim, while his son held a fierce dislike for anything associated with her. Their only connection that he protected as fiercely as the Worthington girl was Crispin. He'd stolen Crispin's devotion from her, and for that reason, she would always thwart him.

However, they were usually insignificant details to irritate him, nothing as major as this. She wasn't foolish not to realize how the impact of her traitorous act would affect their relationship. She needed his acceptance so she could reenter society and claim her standing in the ton. If she didn't secure his approval, then Lady L would strike her vengeance and take no mercy this time around.

"By mistake, my men might have grabbed something of yours and now Lady L has secured your belonging for safekeeping until you can retrieve it."

Ravencroft growled. "Your men?"

Lady Ravencroft forced a laugh between her teeth. "Yes. They thought they were following Lady L's order on kidnapping your brother's bride. Instead, they snagged your betrothed." She held herself still, waiting for his fury.

Ravencroft pinched his lips while his nostrils flared with his contained rage. His gaze narrowed on his mother, watching her squirm in her chair. Because of her thugs' mistake, she risked the very thing she required from him. He refused to grant her the wish of welcoming her back into his life. However, he had dangled the opportunity to keep her in line until he figured out a plan to destroy her and Lady Langdale. Now she gave him a reason to deny her threats. Unfortunately, she still held the key to achieving her goal.

Noel.

He pushed off the door and sat across from his mother. He would need to approach her calmly if he wanted to gain her trust. Ravencroft needed to convince her how he wished for them to find forgiveness with one another. He knew his mother wanted her status to shine amongst the ton more than she wanted to go along with Lady L's revenge. However, he must never underestimate her.

He focused his worried gaze on his mother. "The most important matter is that she is unharmed."

"Yes. Yes," she attempted to reassure him. "Lady L has moved her into my bedchamber, much to my discomfort. We have fed her, and she is well. No harm has come to her person."

Ravencroft bit back his smile when his mother described how Lady L gave Noel her bedchamber. His mother may not have much, but she enjoyed her creature comforts wherever she traveled. He wanted to chuckle at how Noel might react to the lace surrounding her wherever she turned. So far, no harm had befallen her, but the longer she remained under Lady L's hold, the more he questioned her safety.

"I can understand how your men would mistake Noel for Maggie. After all, Noel donned Maggie's clothing in her attempt to pay me a visit. It was foolish of her to wander away from home, so do not be so hard on yourself. The important matter is how I can return Noel to her family."

Lady Ravencroft's head swished back and forth in tight control. "She will not allow you to." She held up her hand for him not to interrupt her. "However, she will allow you to visit the girl to see she is well. Then, after you fulfill the terms of Lady L's request, she will let the girl go free."

This didn't proceed how he imagined it would. His mother wasn't so easily fooled. He must agree to Lady L's terms until he could assess the situation more clearly. After he saw Noel and the layout of Lady Langdale's hideout, he could devise a plan to rescue her.

For now, he must remain a pawn in Lady L's game.

Chapter Seven

RAVENCROFT ROSE TO HIS feet and held out his hand. "Very well. Shall we be off, then?"

Lady Ravencroft accepted his offer with caution. "No argument?"

Ravencroft sighed. "Will it do any good?" When his mother shook her head, he continued. "It is not my livelihood in question to infuriate Lady Langdale. I must think of Noel's welfare first."

His explanation must have satisfied his mother because she told him to follow her. Once inside the carriage, she handed him a blindfold. He tied the fabric over his eyes, and they rode in silence. He understood the procedure and wouldn't fight against it in this instance. Today was about gathering as many clues as he could. He would operate on his own accord, and once he returned home, he would confide in Dracott and the Worthingtons.

Ravencroft kept track of the different turns the carriage took and the sounds outside for clues to their destination. The stench from the river invaded his nostrils, and he realized they were near the docks. However, he was unsure of what end of the river and hoped to gain more clues once they stopped. The carriage slowed to a crawl, and he heard the various shouts from an open market.

While they waited to continue, a whore propositioned the driver. "Only a shilling for a tup. What do you say, guv'na? Come back around for ole' Jane to pleasure ye."

Another clue for Ravencroft to store. Most whores never strayed far from where they spread their thighs at night. He hoped this information would come in handy when he brought Dracott back to find Noel.

The carriage started traveling again. After turning right twice, they stopped. He heard the door open and the swish of his mother's skirts as she disembarked. "Come along, Ravencroft."

Before he stepped out of the carriage, a pair of hands yanked him out and hauled him forward. He didn't need to see who enabled him. He smelt the rankled breath of his mother's thug Horace, smothering him with his force. His meaty hands moved to the back of Ravencroft's neck and squeezed. Ravencroft gritted his teeth and rolled his hands into fists. He wanted to pummel the brute but held back. Soon he would seek his revenge for every brutal attack he had suffered and the torment Horace had inflicted on Dracott for years.

After Horace threw him into a room, his mother tugged off the blindfold. "I have no clue what happened between you two that enrages his temper when he sets eyes on you."

Ravencroft glared at the brute, and Horace returned the glare, puffing out his chest to showcase his strength. The guard might be all steel and force, but Ravencroft would exploit his weakness when needed.

"Please take a seat, Lord Ravencroft," Lady L demanded from the corner.

He turned toward the sound of her voice and saw her glide out from the darkness like a spider moving toward her prey. It was a game she played with him. She enjoyed toying with his emotions, and he took pleasure from refusing her every ploy to coax him to her bed. He may enjoy a woman skilled in the arts of pleasuring him in and out of bed, but he refused to allow her to sink her claws into him. How Worthington had allowed this woman into his life was beyond him.

Ravencroft moved to the nearest chair and sat as she commanded. This brought a smile to her face. He would follow every command until he secured Noel's safe return home. He couldn't allow his temper to rule his behavior, no matter how much they provoked him.

"Thank you for calling on us today."

Ravencroft brushed off a piece of lint from his trousers. "You did not leave me much of a choice."

A devious smile lit Lady L's face. "No, I suppose we did not. The chit must mean more to you than I thought. I should have threatened to kidnap her, had I known how willing you would be to cooperate with my plan. From my observations, I thought you only played the part of a devoted fiancé. I found your act very believable. Especially with such a flighty debutante. I am only curious about how you never went mad while in her company. You must admit, she is not your usual flavor."

Ravencroft's gaze traveled around the room in an act of boredom at Lady L's long, windy opinion of his relationship with Noel. He hoped he fooled her with his act of indifference. It was vital to his plan to show he held no tender emotion for Noel, except for the means to fill his empty coffers. If Lady L sniffed out any sort of interest, she would make Noel suffer during her kidnapping with her destructive mind games. Noel was sharper than most assumed, but she was no match for Lady Langdale.

"You are correct, my lady. You are aware of the type of woman I prefer to warm my bed with. However, Noel Worthington fits perfectly into my plans for a wife." Ravencroft ticks off the reasons on his fingers. "First, she is a beauty to gaze upon. Second, she never questions my word. Third, she never makes demands but seeks for me to make all decisions. The fourth reason is how clueless she is to my other activities. And number five, the most important of all, my marriage to her will secure my finances for life. Worthington is more than generous with Lady Noel's dowry."

"Mmm," Lady L murmured, walking behind him and trailing the tips of her fingers across his shoulders. "I wonder where Worthington has amassed his fortune. While I was his mistress, gossip circulated about his demise. It seems when his father died, he left the family dissolute."

Ravencroft stayed relaxed as she touched him. "He married well. In fact, didn't he throw you over for the Duke of Colebourne's niece? Lady Evelyn was quite a catch for Worthington. Another lady who is a pleasure to gaze upon."

Lady L's fingers pressed harder at his subtle poke. "From what I heard, it was a forced marriage because his wife duped him."

Ravencroft shrugged. "Either way, they must have settled their differences. They are the picture of marital bliss."

"Enough about Worthington," Lady L snapped.

Ravencroft sat forward in the chair. "Then let us discuss the reason for my visit. What can I do to guarantee Lady Noel's release?"

"You are here to fulfill your mother's repayment of the debt she owes me. Also, you and your brother took my possession without my permission, and for that, you must repay me in kind. If you complete your task, I will clear the debt from your entire family."

"A person is not a possession," Ravencroft stated.

"Ahh, but Ren is mine. You and Dracott would be wise to remember that," Lady L warned.

He sliced his hand through the air. Once again, they strayed from the topic that needed to be discussed. He could not care less about the girl they had stolen from Lady L. His concern was Noel and no one else.

"What is the task?" Ravencroft asked.

"The same as before. I need the blueprints to Worthington's townhome."

"I cannot find them," Ravencroft reminded her.

"Then Lady Noel's visit is perfect. I will allow you time with her every day to learn the layout of her home. Over a few days, you will provide me with the drawings to help set my plan into action."

She confused Ravencroft. "Why can I not spend a whole day with her and draw them at my home?"

"Because you must learn to never cross me again. And to do that, I must teach you a lesson. I want the Worthington family to worry over their missing sister and for you to face them with the knowledge of her safety, yet be unable to tell them anything. You will commit another act of betrayal. They will never trust you after her return." Lady L laughed over her brilliant idea.

Ravencroft pretended to ponder her offer over by not responding right away. He started tapping his foot in agitation. "You are sabotaging my plans for the future. Release the girl and I will give you my promise to secure the drawings in a week's time."

Lady L narrowed her gaze, attempting to determine if he spoke the truth. When her gaze drilled into him, he shifted in his chair. He understood what her expression meant and shuddered at what her counteroffer might be. When she sashayed over to him, swinging her hips seductively, he had his answer.

It was quite sad to watch her. The passage of time had been an unkind friend to Barbara Langdale. She kept the wrinkles hidden under layers of face paint. Her exile had advanced her age to a worn-out lady. Her attractiveness faded compared to someone as beautiful as Noel. During her prime, Lady Langdale had been one of the most sought-after widows of the ton. Now she was a middle-aged lady who survived on sheer wit and luck alone. However, since her return to England, she had grown careless, making mistakes that would cost her in the end.

Lost in his musings, Ravencroft was unprepared for her to plop down on his lap. She proceeded to drape across him, running her fingers through his hair. He tried untangling himself from her grasp, but she clung to him. Her attempt was either out of desperation or an attempt to entice him into her bed.

"I will release the girl if you join me in my bedchamber for a night of pleasure. My room is next to hers. After she listens to me cry out your name in passion throughout the night, I will send her on her way home. That is, after your mother leaves the door open to Lady Noel's room and I forget to close mine. Nothing like shocking her innocence away while I get my revenge." She finished her suggestion by palming his cock. However, her eyes widened when she found a man who held no desire at her suggestion.

Ravencroft growled at her boldness and stood, dropping her at his feet. "Show me the girl so I can verify her safety. Then your men can deliver me home, where I will wait for your summons again."

Lady L glared at him but rose to her feet with an elegance he didn't expect. "You are in no position to make demands."

"Am I not? I could refuse your demands, and then what? You would have no way to gain access to Worthington's home," Ravencroft threatened.

"What about your precious fiancée? Do you not care about her welfare if you refuse my offer?"

Ravencroft shrugged. "At this point, not at all. I would like to be on my way since we haven't agreed to any terms."

"Fine," Lady L snarled. She stomped to the door, threw it open, and ordered her guard, "Deliver him to the girl and wait outside."

Ravencroft followed the guard to the second floor, noting the layout of the house as he went. There were only two floors and every door remained closed, so he couldn't detect what rooms they were. The guard stopped at the end of the hallway. They would have an advantage from wherever they entered because of the location of Noel's room. Once he stepped inside, he would get a better layout to stage a rescue.

The guard stepped to the side to allow Ravencroft to enter the bedchamber. He had hoped to slip inside without Noel noticing, but the brute shoved him inside and slammed the door. Once he recovered from the brutality, he searched for Noel, expecting her to defend herself. Instead, she lay on the bed, surrounded by blankets and pillows made from lace. When he moved closer, he came to a stop, shocked at the gown she adorned her body with. Where had she found such a garment?

Every sinful thought Ravencroft could imagine flashed before him, one after another. She was sin personified. A temptress luring him into her decadent paradise. Her breasts spilled from the gown, with her nipples peeking from the silk, offering their delights to him. Noel let out a soft moan and shifted on the bed. Her leg curled up toward her stomach, showing him every kissable inch of temptation. As his cock swelled with need, he groaned and reached down to ease the ache but only grew harder.

Ravencroft glanced over his shoulder and saw the chair propped against the wall. He retraced his steps, staying as quiet as possible, and hooked the chair under the doorknob. It should prevent the guard from entering until he covered Noel from his view. When he turned around, Noel had awakened. She stared at him with the same expression as when he had kissed her.

It spoke of her desires. Her need. Her curiosity. When her eyes lowered, heavy with desire, and she licked her lips, Ravencroft became a doomed man.

"Ah, hell," he muttered.

He strode to the bed and drew her into his embrace. He dipped his head to her neck and sucked on her with greed. Ravencroft took a deep breath, trying to pull himself together before he stole her innocence in this tawdry place.

"Are you in my dream?" Noel whispered.

Ravencroft teased the strap of her gown up and down her arm. "Do you dream of me often?"

Noel pressed closer against him. "Yes. Except this dream was different."

He brushed a kiss to her shoulder. "How so?"

Noel melted in Ravencroft's embrace. When she awakened, she had expected depression to set in over her circumstances. Instead, Ravencroft had stood before her, holding his cock, and it stirred her wanton imagination to life. She wanted to whisper in his ear how her dreams before had been tame compared to the sinful dream she just had. She gasped as his hand closed over her breast, brushing the silk to the side. Her head lowered, and she watched him slide her nipples between his fingers. The motion hypnotized her and lulled her into his seduction.

"Would you like me to draw your nipples into my mouth while my tongue lashes against them before I scrape them between my teeth and suck like a greedy man?" Ravencroft asked her as he pinched one, and Noel whimpered. "Tell me, my love, of your desires. If my hand slides between your cunny, will I find you drenched with your need?"

Noel didn't know if it was the gown that gave her the courage or the unknown of her kidnapping that she dared to answer his question about her dream. "I am drenched, waiting for your touch. However, my dreams were more sinful."

When she whispered her answer, Ravencroft needed no other encouragement. His hand slid into her wetness, and he moaned at the truth of her declaration. He slid a finger deep inside and pressed his thumb to her nub. A moan ripped through the air. Only he held no clue whose it was.

"Tell me about your dream," Ravencroft ordered in a ragged moan.

Noel had forgotten her dream. She could only focus on how Ravencroft played her body like a fine instrument. With each strum of his finger, her body rose another pitch. As pleasurable as his caresses were, her body felt strung tight with an unbearable ache. She needed . . .

Noel's body sang to Ravencroft with a melody he wanted to capture in his soul. He wanted to fulfill every fantasy she held. Make her dreams come true with passion swirling around them.

"Was your dream as sinful as this?" He slid another finger into her tight channel. When she didn't answer him and only moaned, he pulled out his fingers.

Noel's body protested at Ravencroft's withdrawal. Her eyes widened with a desperation she couldn't speak. When he drew his fingers between his lips and sucked off her wetness with a slowness to melt time, a rush of heat consumed her. Her breasts grew heavy, and her nipples tightened into an unbearable ache. She felt herself spiraling out of control with a need unknown to her. Since he joined her on the bed, he had never once kissed her, but Noel drowned in his very touch alone.

"Kiss me," Noel begged.

"Where, love? Did I kiss you in your dreams?"

Noel nodded, whimpering with a need only he could fulfill.

"Tell me where." Ravencroft's voice deepened with his demand as his fingers teased her breasts again.

Noel's breathing quickened when Ravencroft pressed his hardness against her hip. His question from the previous evening prompted her to divulge the secret of her dreams. She boldly grabbed his hand and guided it down her body and slid their fingers back into her wet core.

"Here," she whispered in his ear. "You had spread my thighs apart and kissed me here." She pressed his fingers to her clit. "Your tongue caressed me with soft slow strokes."

Ravencroft was amazed he hadn't come in his pants. Noel's bold declaration took hold of his sanity and shred it into a million pieces. It was in this moment he realized how he had fooled himself into believing she wasn't a threat to his heart all these months.

After she confessed her wanton dream, Noel had never felt so free. She had repressed her desires for him since he never showed interest in her other than presenting himself as a devoted fiancé. She didn't want to scare him away with her forbidden thoughts. However, they only seemed to entice him.

Ravencroft growled his response to her decadent wish and slid down her body. He spread her thighs apart like she described and dove in to devour her sweetness. She might have dreamed of the soft slow strokes of his tongue, but she had unleashed the passion he kept tempered. He could no longer hold his emotions at bay with Noel. She had awakened his dying soul with her passion.

Noel sank onto the scratchy lace and moaned in pleasure. The onslaught of Ravencroft's kisses sent her reeling into the unknown. He dominated her with each stroke of his tongue and demanded her to succumb to his desires. Her legs shook from the powerful force of her need he drew forth with his lips. She gripped his shoulders and pressed into his mouth as her body shook with the aftermath of her desire. Slowly, her body sank back onto the bed and her legs relaxed around his shoulders. Noel hummed her pleasure as Ravencroft placed the softest of kisses on her thighs. She floated as her body recovered from the passion they shared.

Ravencroft lay with his head on her thigh and fought for control as her fingers brushed through his hair. His cock ached, needing to release itself between her thighs, but he fought his desire. Noel's soft hum calmed his soul, and he regained his senses.

"Ravencroft?"

He chuckled. Even after what they had just shared, she still addressed him so formally. He would enjoy teaching her lessons in intimacies. He lifted his head, met her eyes, and slid a finger back inside her. "You may call me Gregory when we are intimate, if you so desire."

Noel's eyes widened, and she gulped, nodding. "Gregory?"

"Yes, love?" he asked before dipping his head to drag his tongue across her folds. She tasted too sweet to stop, even though he must.

"I . . . umm . . . That is . . ." Noel closed her eyes as Ravencroft—no, Gregory started his sweet torture again. Her body hummed back to life.

Ravencroft chuckled at her confusion. With one last lick, he pulled away before he took her in his arms and ravished her until she screamed from the rafters, letting her captors know who she surrendered to. He drew her gown around her legs and covered her breasts. He wanted to draw her into his arms, but it wasn't the wisest course of action. So he rolled off the bed to his feet and put distance between them. She was too tempting of a distraction, one he must resist.

The door rattled, and Ravencroft realized their time had ended. Noel squeaked and reached for a blanket to cover herself with. When the guard started pounding on the door, he grabbed Noel's clothes and threw them at her.

"Change your clothes now," he ordered and strode over to the door. "Give me two more minutes. The lady is getting dressed."

The guard grunted his permission of the request. Ravencroft strode back over to Noel. She had already changed and was stuffing the gown back into the wardrobe. He had many questions concerning her state of dress, but they would wait until later. Now he must reassure her before they forced him to leave.

Ravencroft gripped Noel by her shoulders. "Are you well?"

Noel nodded.

"I must leave you here, but Lady L has granted her permission for my return tomorrow. In the meantime, I plan to rescue you from her clutches. Do not argue with her or my mother. Stay silent. Can you do that?"

Noel nodded again.

He pressed his forehead against hers. He didn't know what to make of her silence. Did she regret their time together? Was she ashamed?

The guard banged on the door. "Now!"

"Just a minute more," Ravencroft shouted back. "Damn. I wanted to explain everything to you. But I must leave. Here, take this." He pressed a pocketknife into her hand. Then he kissed her forehead, stalked to the door, and removed the chair.

Noel watched Lady L drag Ravencroft from the room. She ran after him, but the guard locked the door. After pressing her ear to the panel, she only heard footsteps stomping away. She turned around, stomping her own feet in frustration. The boarded windows prevented Noel from seeing if Ravencroft left her to her own demise. Her gaze landed on the bed, and she pressed her hand on the wall to steady herself. Their time together came rushing back, and she couldn't believe her scandalous behavior. Her cheeks warmed as she remembered the confession she had made to Ravencroft. Or Gregory, as he had teased her.

She moved to the bed and sat down. Her hand ran over the lacy cover, and she swore Ravencroft's heat singed her fingertips. He had swept in like a whirlwind and departed just as swiftly, leaving Noel adrift in confusion. She didn't understand what to think of his visit or his cryptic comments. As for his order not to provoke his mother or Lady L, it was unnecessary. She wasn't a dimwit and understood the severity if she should. Yet, after her confinement in this bedchamber, she held on to her temper by a thin thread. It was in her nature to avoid conflict, and she preferred to see the positivity in every situation. However, there wasn't anything positive about her kidnapping.

And why did Ravencroft want her to stay silent toward Lady Langdale? Did he fear the lady would reveal more of their relationship? Noel wasn't naïve not to realize they shared something. She hadn't noticed it when he swept her into a passionate embrace, but she'd caught the fragrance when he held her to him before he left. The musky scent had clung to his suit coat. And she wasn't blind to see the face paint smeared on his collar. Which only left Noel to wonder if Ravencroft played a game with her affections?

And if so, for what prize?

Chapter Eight

ONCE AGAIN, RAVENCROFT SAT blindfolded, oblivious to his surroundings on his return home. At least, his mother didn't join him for the return trip, and the guard rode with the driver. He would attempt to jump from the carriage, but they had bound his wrists. Which left him to count the turns and listen for any sounds that would help him locate the hideout later.

He had to scratch his plan to sneak in through the windows to Noel's room since they had boarded them. After he saw the house they sequestered her in, his need to rescue Noel became more urgent. At least he gave her a weapon to protect herself with, if she needed it. He hoped they never gave her a reason to.

The carriage started again, and Ravencroft swayed back and forth, trying to remain on the seat. It wasn't much longer when the carriage stopped again and the door opened. The guard undid his hands but kept the shield in place.

"Wait until you no longer hear the carriage, then you can remove the mask," the guard ordered.

Ravencroft bowed. "At your command."

His insolence earned him a smack against the head. However, Ravencroft no longer cared. It was the last command he would obey from them. He must attempt to rescue Noel this evening because he refused to have her endure another minute in their capture.

After he no longer heard the carriage, he swept off the mask and strode into his house. He would need to send word to Dracott. Ravencroft hated to interrupt his honeymoon, but he needed his help. And all because he had failed to secure their freedom from his mother's and Lady L's clutches. He decided from this moment forth he would use Dracott's resources. Even if it meant allowing the Worthingtons to take over.

When he held Noel in his embrace earlier, he had realized how selfish it was for him to attempt her rescue on his own. She didn't deserve to suffer because of his pride. Sometimes a man must place the welfare of others before himself. And securing Noel's safety was that moment for him.

"Meg, find me someone to run a message," Ravencroft ordered once he strolled inside his home.

"Yes, my lord. You have . . . That is . . ." Meg stuttered.

Ravencroft paused, noting Meg's discomfort. "What is the matter?" he asked calmly. He didn't want to frighten off the few servants he had.

"I tried to stop them, but they insisted they would wait." Meg pointed to his study.

Ravencroft sighed. He didn't need to question who had invaded his home. Meg's nervousness explained her behavior. "You did fine. I have decided to leave town for a few days. You may inform the other servants to take a week to themselves. There is no sense why any of you shouldn't enjoy the time off during my absence. Please inform the other servants to return to work this time next week."

"Oh, thank you, my lord. You are so kind. I would enjoy a visit with my family. Can we get you anything before we leave?" Meg gushed.

"No need." He smiled at her as though he didn't have a care in the world. The complete opposite of how he truly felt. However, it was brilliant of him to send them away. His home wasn't safe, and he didn't want to risk their innocent lives because of the danger he was involved in. Especially when he was about to double-cross Lady Langdale.

He waited for Meg to scamper off before he went to his study. Once there, he saw how everyone had made themselves comfortable, waiting for him. At least he didn't have to locate Dracott. It appeared Worthington had already interrupted the newlyweds' honeymoon.

Ravencroft strolled in and made his way to Maggie. He always sensed her dislike, and the frown on her face showed she felt no differently. He held out his hand. "May I offer my congratulations on your marriage to my brother and also my apology for pulling you away from your honeymoon?"

Maggie narrowed her gaze before taking his hand. "Thank you. There is no need to apologize for Noel's disappearance unless you orchestrated it."

After giving her hand a friendly squeeze, he dropped his hand. "No, I did not. However, it was my mother's guards who stole her, and for that, I am responsible."

"We both are," Dracott spoke from behind him.

Ravencroft turned. "They thought they grabbed Maggie since Noel had adorned herself in breeches."

Dracott nodded. "That makes sense."

"Breeches!" Eden exclaimed. "Noel in breeches? You must be mistaken."

Ravencroft shook his head. "No. I am not."

Maggie laughed. "Now that I would love to see. Especially since she always nagged me about how proper it was to dress like a lady. What would prompt her to dress like a hoyden?"

Ravencroft winced. He knew the exact reason and must tell them if he wanted them to trust him. His natural reaction was to lie and send them on their way on a false hunt to find Noel. However, if he wanted any future with Noel, then he must admit every dishonest act he had committed since coming into their lives. And he wanted nothing more than a future with Noel, one spent exploring the passion they had only just begun to explore.

"My fault again. On the night of your wedding, she snuck over here."

"And you neglected to mention this earlier, why?" Worthington growled.

Ravencroft sighed. "Because I thought I could handle this on my own."

Worthington advanced on Ravencroft. "That was not your decision to make. As of this moment, I rescind my permission for you to marry Noel."

"I agree. However, with all due respect, you will not decide the fate of our engagement. That is Noel's decision only." Ravencroft stood tall with his hands behind his back.

Worth stepped between the two gentlemen and pulled his brother back. "Instead of working against each other, let us work together to bring Noel home."

Ravencroft nodded his agreement, at peace with Worthington if the other gentleman would agree to a truce. Worthington kept glaring at him but gave a slight nod to indicate he agreed. Ravencroft moved to sit behind his desk while the other gentlemen settled in a chair.

"Tell us what you know," Worth urged.

"They are holding Noel in their hideout." He held up his hand when Worthington opened his mouth to interrupt him. "I have no clue where because they blindfolded me for the ride. Once I reached the hideout, Lady L gave me the ultimatum of helping her secure the layout of your townhome or harming Noel. I agreed to help her in exchange for Noel's freedom once I secured the documents she needed."

"Do you know why she wants them?" Eden asked.

"She planned a heist during Maggie's debutante ball. Since Maggie will no longer have one because of her marriage, Lady L will strike during our wedding. She seeks her revenge by causing you misery when she attacks the ton. You will have to deal with the aftermath when the ton blames you for their losses." Ravencroft directed his stare at Worthington.

"Why now?" Worthington asked.

"Because over the years, she has grown her force. She believes she can infiltrate England and seek her revenge. You became an enemy to her after you threw her over for Evelyn. She expected you to marry her. When Colebourne put a bounty on her head, she ran to the Continent and plotted her revenge," Ravencroft explained.

"I never gave her any sign of a marriage proposal. She only suited one purpose, and it was foolish on my part to have ever gotten involved with her. Especially once I learned of her pastime. As for Colebourne, she picked the wrong peer to double-cross," Worthington stated.

"How does she plan to secure the blueprints?" asked Worth.

Ravencroft rubbed a hand across his face to ease his stress from having to explain this next part. He knew the Worthington men would object, but it was crucial they play along with Lady L's plans. "Each day going forth, they will force me back to their hideout. While I'm there, I am to earn Noel's trust and coax her to tell me about any special nuances that only a member of your family would have knowledge of. Any broken locks, squeaky doors, secret passageways. Anything to help her cause. This routine will proceed every day until Lady L has what she requires."

Dracott snarled in disgust. "Was part of the threat for you to pretend ignorance of Noel's whereabouts to the Worthingtons?"

Ravencroft nodded. "Yes. She wants my relationship with Noel and her family to suffer for her revenge against us for what we did last year."

Dracott humphed. "Her terror will never end, will it?"

His comment was more of an observation than a question. They both knew Lady L would forever seek her vindication as long as she remained free. Ravencroft finally understood why his brother wanted them to join forces with Worth and Ralston to bring Lady L to justice. They never held a chance at ending this on their own. They needed an arsenal of men to bring her down. Ravencroft exchanged a look with Dracott, telling him he accepted his demands.

Dracott nodded, then turned to Worth. "How do you want to handle this?"

Worth looked between the brothers, trying to decipher their exchange. "Do I have both of your cooperation to follow my demands?"

"Yes," both men agreed.

Worth sighed. "As much as this should stay within our family, it cannot. We will need help from those we can trust to stop this lady from destroying those we love. We must confide in Ralston, Kincaid, and Falcone."

"Are you sure we can trust Lord Falcone?" Eden bit out.

Everyone turned toward Eden at her objection. She tried to keep a serious expression on her face, so her family didn't notice her discomfort at discussing the gentleman. She even fought to keep her gaze from Maggie after she heard her sister snicker.

Ravencroft frowned. "Is there a reason we should not? I don't want anyone involved who will place Noel at more risk."

"I only ask because Ralston and Kincaid are practically family, so I understand needing their guidance. However, Falcone is an outsider," Eden explained.

"I can understand your hesitation. At first I did not trust Falcone when Ralston brought him on. However, over the years, he has proven himself a worthy ally. And right now, we need his help," Worth tried to reassure Eden.

Eden pinched her lips. "Very well."

"She will have men watching my every move," Ravencroft said.

"Then we shall give them something to report back. We will host a small dinner party this evening, inviting the Ralstons, Kincaids, and Lord Falcone. Ravencroft, you will arrive as usual to keep up the pretense Lady L wishes for. During dinner, we will discuss how to rescue Noel and how we should proceed with the investigation." Worth looked at each person before making his last statement. "Also, we will put aside our differences and work together to achieve Noel's safe return."

Everyone murmured their agreement.

"Dracott and I will go into the office and invite the gentlemen to dinner. Reese, you need to escort the ladies home, where both of you will remain." Worth looked at his sisters. "Ravencroft, proceed about your day as usual. We must all appear that we are in great distress over Noel's disappearance."

Ravencroft nodded. He looked at Worthington and noted the earl appeared satisfied with his brother's command. It was highly unusual for an older brother to take a step back and allow a younger sibling to lead. However, that wasn't the case with the Worthingtons. They held trust and respect with one another, the same as he held with Dracott. However, his foolish pride had kept him from listening to his brother's advice.

Ravencroft rose from behind his desk to escort his guests out since he had sent the servants off on a break. "I shall join your family at dinner."

Worthington glanced around. "Where are your servants?"

"I sent them away for a week because I wished no harm to come upon them. It does not matter much because I only retain a few servants," Ravencroft explained.

Worthington arched a brow. "Because of your financial difficulties?"

"Reese, that is enough," Maggie interjected.

"That is all right, my lady. Your brother is correct. I will be honest, I only sought Noel's hand because of her dowry and how easily manageable she would be for a wife. However, after I have become better acquainted with your sister, my feelings have changed dramatically," Ravencroft explained.

Maggie gazed at him shrewdly and then nodded, offering him a smile. "Yes, our Noel has that ability to change one's mind."

Ravencroft smiled back. "That she does."

Worthington grunted, then led his sisters away. Worth slapped him on the back in a silent show of appreciation at his reply. He glanced over his shoulder and noticed Dracott leaning against the wall, waiting for him. He tilted his head at Worth, and Dracott shook his head in reply. Ravencroft closed the door after Worth and followed Dracott back into the study. He found his brother already pouring them a drink.

Dracott took a drink before he sat down. "At least they did not question us about what we did to entice Lady L's wrath."

Ravencroft settled next to him, stretching out his legs. "Do not think they won't. Your employer will inquire when it is pertinent to do so."

"You have a point. Now, what can you describe about your visit?" Dracott asked.

Ravencroft set the glass off to the side, not taking a sip. "The stench is strong, and I believe the house is located near the wharf. Also, look for a streetwalker by the name of Jane. She calls out to hackney drivers. I don't believe I rode in a carriage of wealth but one for hire by the comfort of it." He continued with the details of his trip and what he had overheard while trapped in the carriage.

Dracott finished his drink and stood up. "I'll see what I can uncover before dinner this evening. In the meantime, prepare yourself for the unexpected. We both know Lady L won't follow through with what she laid out. She will deviate from her plan when her men escort you back to Noel. I will warn Worth and have Kincaid's men follow at a discreet distance."

"I agree. Tomorrow cannot come soon enough. We both know what Noel might endure under their watch. Whatever we plan, we must do so with haste."

Dracott pointed at Ravencroft's drink. "Calm yourself. This will soon be over."

After Dracott left, he stared at the drink. He refused to take a swallow. He could mark two occasions when he had overindulged in alcohol to settle his emotions, and they had both ended in disaster. The first was when he encountered his mother years after she abandoned him and drew him into her destruction with Lady Langdale. The second was the night Noel visited him. And because of that, she was now a victim of Lady L's revenge. No. He refused to take another drink while they kept Noel captive.

Never again would he lose himself because of his inability to face his emotions.

Chapter Nine

WHILE NOEL FINISHED EATING her lunch, Lady L strolled inside her cell. Her description was dramatic, but with the windows bordered and nothing to occupy her time, it felt like a prison. Not to mention the locked door and the guard standing outside. How else would one refer to her demise?

"Are you enjoying your stay?" Lady L sauntered around the room, picking up a trinket, then setting it back down.

Noel wiped her mouth. "Mmm. How should one feel when forced against their will to remain a prisoner?"

Lady L let out a devious chuckle. "You are cleverer than I thought. I must take that into consideration."

"Consideration for what?"

Lady L waved a hand in the air. "Oh, nothing for you to concern yourself over. Your only concern is if you are presentable enough for Lord Ravencroft. There must be a garment in Lady Ravencroft's wardrobe you wish to change into to please him."

Warmth washed over Noel. She didn't need to glance in the mirror to know she blushed a fiery red. "The lady owns nothing I wish to wear."

Lady L smiled at the girl's discomfort and found immense pleasure in watching her squirm. She opened the wardrobe and pushed the garments around. She knew what Lady Ravencroft kept for clothing and wanted to embarrass the chit. "Are you sure?" Her eyebrows lifted. "Lord Ravencroft finds pleasure in such decadence. I only thought you would want to please him."

Noel's gaze narrowed. "Lord Ravencroft is none of your concern."

Lady L threw her head back and laughed. "Oh, you are feistier than I imagined, too. Very unpredictable from your usual behavior. Has Ravencroft ever seen this side of your character? If so, I do not believe he would've continued with the engagement. Your behavior is quite the opposite of what he wishes for in a wife, considering he prefers a lady who is placid. Well, it is better this is coming to light before you share wedding vows with him."

"You seem under the impression you know my betrothed quite well. My question is, how well?" Noel asked.

"A question you must ask Ravencroft. A lady does not . . . well . . . how should I phrase this? Kiss and tell? No. That is too tame of a description for what Ravencroft and I share."

Noel held herself still. Tiny pricks of tears stabbed at her eyes, begging to fall. Noel took a deep breath to keep her doubts at bay. She held enough suspicions of his involvement with the lady, but she refused to believe they held an intimate connection with one another. She decided to follow her mother's advice on staying silent when another person provoked you to attack. To do so only gave them the power over your unstable emotions.

"Will Lord Ravencroft pay a visit today?" Noel asked.

"No, my dear, he will not. However, you shall see him soon. Now if you will follow me, we must move you to new accommodations while you stay in our care. This is no longer a safe environment for your visit. Before long, your brother and his friends will attempt to infiltrate my domain and rescue you. And I cannot allow that to happen until Ravencroft provides me with the information I need. Once I receive what I require, you may return home." Lady L moved toward the door and turned, motioning for Noel to follow her.

Noel followed as instructed. She didn't understand why they had to move her but hoped it gave her a chance to escape. She had found a sewing kit in Lady Ravencroft's chest and sewed a pocket inside her pants to hold the knife Ravencroft gave her. Her shirt billowed around her, hiding the slight bulge.

"Oh, and do not attempt to escape during this transfer. It will only bring about your demise," Lady L threatened.

Noel gulped. The lady might as well add mind reading to her nefarious traits. However, she would follow the lady's order and bide her time to escape after she learned more about her new destination. She only hoped it was possible.

Lady L handed her a blindfold. "Cover your eyes and do not cause trouble for my guards. We will meet again soon." Lady L paused and added with a chuckle, "Give Ravencroft my love."

Noel glared at the lady as she covered her eyes, but it only earned her more of the lady's amusement on her behalf. The guard grabbed Noel by the arm and dragged her outside. The warmth of the air washed over her skin. Noel crinkled her nose when the stench of the Thames invaded her senses. Wherever they took her, she hoped it held better accommodations. The guard tossed her into the back of the carriage, and before she could rip off the blindfold, he tied her hands together in front of her. She snarled her displeasure, ready to scream, when they shoved a rag into her mouth.

They made sure she stayed silent and unable to see where they took her. By moving her, they showed how they feared her family's wrath. Before long, Lady L would meet her demise. In the meantime, Noel must remain patient instead of irritated at becoming Lady L's victim.

Ravencroft should have followed his instinct and raided Lady L's hideout last night. Instead, he had allowed Worth to convince him to follow along with Lady L's plan to make it appear as if she had him cornered. His role was to secure Noel's safety by visiting her each day and drawing out the plans for the townhome, while everyone else followed his trip and learned the layout of Lady L's hideout. Once they had a plan in place, they would attempt to rescue Noel. Key emphasis on attempt because it would amount to no more. They didn't understand the magnitude of secrecy at Lady Langdale's disposal. Her network extended further than they even imagined. They refused to believe what he and Dracott told them.

It didn't surprise him when the carriage took a different route to the hideout. The carriage traveled without delay along the quietness of the countryside, and Ravencroft realized they were taking him to a new destination, leaving him to wonder if Noel would join him or if Lady L had concocted a new plan for her revenge. Either way, the plan they had devised last night wouldn't come to fruition.

Ravencroft sat back in the seat and didn't break the bond around his wrists. It wouldn't do any good because wherever they traveled, they prepared for the unexpected. No sense wearing out his strength until he needed to. He understood what played out because of the part he played in the past when the position was reversed. He would use his knowledge to his advantage and draw upon his patience until he could escape. A trait he had learned to excel at while under Lady L's thumb.

Soon, the carriage came to a stop, and the guard dragged him out. Once his feet landed on the ground, they ripped off his blindfold. The sun blinded him, and he squinted his eyes to look around at his surroundings. When he stood still, the guard shoved at him to keep moving. A cottage was nestled amongst the trees and hidden from the road, with no other homes nearby. They delivered him to an isolated location where he couldn't escape.

He followed the guard into a one-room cottage. There was a bed nestled in one corner. The other corner appeared to be a kitchen area, holding a table and chairs. The rest of the cottage comprised of a sofa, two chairs, and an end table by the fireplace. From the looks of his surroundings, Ravencroft realized they wouldn't allow him to return home. Would they also bring Noel to the cottage?

The guard stepped forward and ripped his knife through Ravencroft's binds. "Do not attempt an escape."

Ravencroft rubbed his wrists. "I would not even dream of doing so."

Before the guard reacted to his sarcastic reply, he wandered away, inspecting the cottage. Besides the door, the only other means of escape was a window facing the road. After settling on a chair, he questioned the guard, "Will you reveal the reason for my arrival in this piece of paradise or must I wait for an explanation?"

The guard sneered. "Still think you are above us, do you?"

Ravencroft lifted his shoulders in indifference. "I do not have to think about what I already know."

The guard growled and advanced toward Ravencroft, but he stopped in his tracks when the door opened. His employer issued commands behind him, and he retreated to Lady L's side. Ravencroft leapt to his feet as they led Noel into the cottage. When he saw how they had trussed her up and gagged her, his wrath exploded. He tore to her side, pulled the rag out, and gently tugged on her restraints, but she only cried out in pain.

"What in the hell is this?" Ravencroft roared.

Noel cringed at his tone, but everyone else found amusement in his frustration. He snarled and held out his hand. After Lady L nodded her acceptance, the guard handed over his knife.

"Keep still. I am going to cut off your restraints." Ravencroft's voice softened into a gentle tone.

Noel's heart rate slowed at Ravencroft's touch. Even though he expressed his fury at her treatment, his nearness calmed her. Her body might shake from the uncertainty, but she wasn't as frightened as she had been on the carriage ride. When the noise from the city lessened and the stillness of the countryside drifted through the window, Noel had feared for her life. With each rut the carriage traveled over, it had tossed Noel from one side of the seat to the other since she couldn't hold on. Her body ached from the uncomfortable ride.

Ravencroft undid the blindfold and drew her into his arms, protecting her from the evilness surrounding them. He tucked her head under his chin and rubbed her back with calming strokes. Noel released a breath she didn't realize she had held. She trembled with a need to cry, but she refused to allow Lady L to see her as a defenseless victim. She pulled away from Ravencroft, denying herself the comfort he offered. In all honesty, she didn't trust Ravencroft any more than she did her captor.

She stepped away from Ravencroft and rubbed her hands up and down her arms, trying to wipe away the chill encasing her body. She glanced around her new holdings and noticed the familiar surroundings. Noel had only visited the cottage on a few occasions, but she remembered the furniture. The only difference was the bed resting in the corner. There was a clue near the window that would reveal if it was the same cottage. However, she wouldn't risk looking until she was alone.

The distance separating him from Noel was but a step away, yet her rejection made it seem far apart. He saw the uncertainty in her eyes change from one emotion to another as she took in her surroundings. Ravencroft wanted to ease her worries, but he couldn't when he didn't understand the reason they were here. He didn't want to show Noel his own fear. As furious as he was at how they had treated her, he also worried over their fate. By driving them to the countryside in what appeared to be a lover's hideaway, it provided Lady L with many options to destroy them. He only hoped their lives remained intact.

"Why are we here?" Ravencroft demanded. "I followed your rules."

"Yes you did, Lord Ravencroft. However, you deviated from them with the dinner party you attended last night." Lady L strolled around the cottage, inspecting it to her satisfaction.

"I only followed your orders. You cannot hold me accountable for the guests the Worthingtons invited to dine with," Ravencroft objected.

"Yet you did more than dine, did you not?" Lady L asked.

Ravencroft sighed. "It does not matter how I answer. You have reached your own conclusion. Now, will you please inform us why you have delivered us to the middle of nowhere?"

Lady L's shrill laughter filled the cottage. "So demanding, but still polite." She moved behind Noel and trailed her fingers across her back. "Do you not find that an attractive trait about our Lord Ravencroft?"

Noel pressed her tongue to the roof of her mouth to keep from biting out an answer, but her resistance failed. "Lord Ravencroft is not ours, but mine."

Her comment only amused Lady Langdale. "So feisty. Mmm, perhaps if you have no use for her after we conclude our business, Ravencroft, I will take her for myself."

A look of horror crossed Noel's face at Lady L's suggestion. Noel's innocence was refreshing, but it hindered her knowledge of the alternative lifestyles other people led. However, in Lady L's case, it was a depraved one she forced others to live while under the influence of drugs. Usually, opium was her preference. He had watched her ruin many lives over the years with her twisted afflictions. Men and women alike, she held no preference for who she destroyed.

Ravencroft closed the step between him and Noel, grabbing her hand. He squeezed it, silently asking her to stay quiet. Lady L only baited them to see how much they meant to each other. While Noel's comment flattered him, it gave Lady L ammunition to know how much he meant to Noel. His holding Noel's hand was a contradiction in itself. He only showed Lady L how he protected his fiancée.

Noel understood Ravencroft's message, but she found it hard to stay silent. She wanted to rant and rave about the injustice of her kidnapping. Lady L infuriated her with her comments about Ravencroft, implying they held a personal intimacy, while she sensed Ravencroft held only contempt for the lady. His tone and mannerism showed how he reined in his temper around Lady Langdale. His actions alone showed how she should proceed with caution. If Ravencroft held himself back, then she should too.

After neither of them spoke anymore, Lady L grew bored. She motioned for her guards to leave before she issued her demands and warning. She waved her arm toward the kitchen area of the cottage. "You have enough provisions to last you for a week. Ravencroft, you will find a drawing pad and pencils to accomplish your task. Lady Noel, your presence here alone will help me achieve part of my revenge. I shall return in a week's time to collect your task"—she pointed at Ravencroft and then at Noel—"and seal your fate. Until then, my lovebirds."

However, before she closed the door, she popped back inside. "Oh, and I have positioned men to guard the cottage. So try not to cause too much trouble for them."

With that, Lady L sauntered to her carriage and left them alone.

Chapter Ten

NOEL NEEDED TO SATISFY her curiosity. She should wait for when Ravencroft didn't observe her every move. However, patience wasn't an admirable trait of hers. It didn't matter anyway because he wouldn't realize what she looked for. Her friend had marked the cottage during her time spent alone with her husband. Gemma Ralston had giggled over her action when she described it. Noel had sighed over the romantic overture Gemma made toward her husband.

She moved around the cottage to accommodate herself with her new prison. Ravencroft kept his gaze fastened on her with every step. She lifted the curtain away from the window, pretending an interest in the outdoors when she noted the heart carved into the window frame with G and B inside. Noel laid her hand over the carving, rubbing her thumb across the grooves in the wooden frame. A sense of security wrapped around her at the sight of the initials carved into the wood. At least she found comfort from the possibility of an escape.

Noel turned to tell Ravencroft the news but stopped herself. He had yet to prove himself worthy of her trust. Even though they had shared a few intimate interludes, doubts of his character still lingered. Lady L's familiarity toward Ravencroft didn't help his favor. She longed for Ravencroft to be Gregory again. Courteous and reliable Gregory who doted on her every word. The man before her now left her feeling uncertain, yet yearning for the passion he stroked to life inside her. His very presence in such close quarters heightened her senses. She wanted nothing more than to run to him and throw herself into his arms.

Her gaze strayed to the bed with longing. She pictured them tangled in the sheets with their limbs intertwined while they made love to one another. His bold caresses stroking her body into an avalanche of desire while his kisses demanded her surrender. Her eyes drifted closed as her thoughts turned into a forbidden frenzy. How would she resist surrendering to the desire that beckoned her toward him?

Ravencroft followed her every movement. She had yet to speak after Lady L departed. Instead, she wandered about the cottage as if it were familiar. Noel stood at the window, rubbing her fingers over the frame, as if she had stood there before. Which was nonsense. Now she stood facing the bed, and her gaze darkened before her eyes closed. Was she imagining them making love? Did she picture him worshipping her body with the softest of kisses while his hands boldly claimed her? He groaned at his fantasy and turned away from her staring at the bed. He rubbed his hand over his cock to ease the ache begging for him to lay Noel on the bed and satisfy his urges. How in the hell would he resist her when her very nearness undid him?

Ravencroft cleared his throat. "Can I get you anything?"

Noel opened her eyes, turning toward Ravencroft. "A way home?"

Ravencroft barked out a laugh. "I thought more along the lines of a cup of tea."

Noel shrugged. "I suppose that will do, for starters."

Ravencroft nodded. "Right." He hesitated like he wanted to say something more but stayed silent.

Noel walked over to the table, staring at the drawing paper and pencils scattered across the top. She stacked them into a pile and moved them over. "Do you need help?"

"No."

Noel sat in a chair, watching Ravencroft make tea. What struck her as odd was how comfortable he appeared performing the simple task. An act most uncommon to find a gentleman of his ranking doing. "May I ask how you learned to make tea?"

Ravencroft glanced up from pouring the steaming water out of the kettle into cups. "Before my father passed away, the number of servants we employed had dwindled down to a handful. When we couldn't afford to pay them, they left. Except for the butler who had been with our family since my father was a lad. He taught me how to survive on the basics of life." He paused, smiling at her. "Making tea being one of the necessary survival techniques. Then, when I located my mother and saw how Dracott lived, I refused to leave him alone in those conditions. Since he refused to leave, I stayed, and Dracott taught me a few more techniques in order to survive."

Noel took the cup he offered her and sipped on the brew. While he told of his skills, he had flavored her tea the way she liked, without her even realizing it. "Mmm, delicious."

Ravencroft smiled over her pleasure. "I apologize for the lengthy explanation."

Noel reached for his hand. "No. I appreciate your honesty. Also, I wish to learn everything there is about you."

Noel was sincere in her statement. She might hold a few doubts about Ravencroft, but she still held a profound affection for him. To understand him, she needed every detail about the true Gregory Ravencroft, not the gentleman he had portrayed himself to be since she met him.

He linked his fingers through hers, glancing around the cottage. "It would appear you will get your wish for the next week at least."

"Only for a week?" Noel glanced at him out of the corner of her eye.

"A lifetime if you still wish to," Ravencroft murmured with hope.

"Mmm. We shall see how this week progresses." She lifted the cup to hide how her lips lifted into a teasing smile.

He stood there, unsure how to respond to Noel. He couldn't tell if she was serious or if she teased him. Her expression gave nothing away to show him the temperament of her mood. She set her cup down and pointed at him to take a seat next to her. He followed her command, waiting for her to ask her questions. And she didn't disappoint him. Noel fired them at him all at once, not drawing a breath until she finished. And throughout the entire tirade, she still held onto his hand.

"What is the task assigned to you? How is my stay in this cottage going to help Lady L seek her revenge? What is your relationship with that woman? Have you made love to her before? Why does she insinuate knowledge of such intimate details about your preferences in the bedroom? Why did your mother's men kidnap me? How is that obnoxious woman even your mother? Do I have to claim her as a mother-in-law? I understand that is horrible of me to ask, but I must know. Why has my family not rescued me? Why did you leave me in their clutches yesterday?" Noel finished her questions with a sob.

"Ah, love." Ravencroft drew Noel into his arms and carried her over to the sofa. She cried her heart out, drenching his shirt with her tears. He tried to soothe her with comforting words, but the strength she had held firmly together for the past few days crumbled all around them. She clung to him one moment, then she balled her hands into fists and beat against his chest the next.

After she calmed down, the only sound in the cottage was her sniffles. They tore at Ravencroft's soul. He wished he was a stronger man who had prevented the torture she endured. From this day forth, he wouldn't allow anyone to dictate his actions. They would escape this hell, and no one would ever stand in their path again.

Noel had every right to hold onto her fury at him for abandoning her. At the time, he had thought he acted in a way that was best for her safety. But, in fact, his actions were a result of not defying his mother and Lady L because he was a coward. Well, no more. Noel came first and foremost and everyone else could go hang.

Ravencroft drew the blanket from the back of the sofa and tucked it around Noel before he answered every single one of her questions. "My task is to draw the layout of your townhome. Since I never secured the blueprints for Lady L in the timely manner she allotted me, she has forced us into this proximity. I am to use my charms to trick you into revealing the secrets of your home."

"Why does she want the layout of our home?"

Ravencroft rubbed a strand of Noel's hair between his fingers. "Because she plans to strike a heist during our wedding ceremony."

Noel bit at her bottom lip. "What if there is no wedding ceremony?"

"To answer your next question, she plans to expose our stay in this beautiful cottage to the ton. I haven't figured out how, but I am sure it will involve my mother somehow. Which leaves you as a ruined lady unless we wed."

Noel gasped. "Why would your own mother be party to such a devious act against us?"

"On to your next set of questions. My mother only looks out for herself and no other. As far as how I am her child, I guess God wanted to play a cruel trick or teach me a lesson about human nature. I am still unsure of that. My offer of marriage will stand for an eternity. And if you decide to accept it, then you never have to claim her as your mother-in-law. I hope when your brother destroys Lady L, he also destroys my mother, too. Once they capture her and she is no longer part of our lives and Dracott's, the better it will be."

"Was her purpose for taking me to play into Lady L's plan?" Noel asked.

"No. Since you dressed yourself in boy's clothing, they assumed it was Maggie who Lady L had ordered kidnapped in the first place," Ravencroft explained.

"Why were they so set on kidnapping Maggie?"

Ravencroft sighed. "Because Dracott's desertion from the thievery ring infuriated Lady L more than mine. She wanted to make him suffer for leaving and for helping another person escape. She watched how attached Dracott was becoming to Maggie and knew if she kidnapped her, she would lure him into returning for Maggie's freedom."

"The lady is more complex than I thought." A shudder racked Noel's body, and Ravencroft drew her tighter against him. "I cannot imagine Reese with such a lady."

"In your brother's defense, it was during a time he was at his lowest and she charmed him into believing she was something she wasn't."

"Ugh. Either way, I am so thankful Evelyn came into his life. To imagine our lives saddled with that woman."

Ravencroft chuckled. "I do not believe your brother would've ever offered for her. Which is the reason for her revenge against your family. She will find immense pleasure if she can ruin your good name."

Noel toyed with the buttons on his shirt. "Have you ever been at your lowest with her?"

Ravencroft tipped Noel's head up and gazed into her eyes. "*No.*" He spoke the one word with emphasis to make it clear to her. "I have never bedded that woman, nor have I ever desired to. I will not lie to you. Over the years, and even yesterday, she has attempted to seduce me. My answer has always been no. She only pretends to know what I prefer. She baits you with her words because she finds pleasure in upsetting you, while she has no clue what I desire in my bed. She is jealous of you, Noel. And it is pure jealousy that fuels her desire for revenge." His explanation came out in a passionate denial, forcing Noel to understand how she was a threat to Lady Langdale.

Noel's eyes widened. "Oh."

"As to the type of lady I desire to warm my bed, I am quite selective."

Noel gulped before squeaking out, "How so?"

"First of all, nothing strikes my interest more than a highly intelligent lady. Not a bluestocking who always has to prove her intelligence. But one who enjoys the simplicity of life while understanding the circumstances surrounding her. Who is always aware but has no need to flaunt herself."

His hand ran through her tresses as he continued. "One whose beauty is simple but very understated because she is unaware of her sexuality and the power she yields over the gentleman she has captured under her spell."

Ravencroft only meant to reassure Noel of his affections from the damage Lady L had inflected with her destructive taunts, not to stroke his own desires. But when Noel's body melted into his and her soft little sighs escaped when he touched her, he ached to kiss her lips again and show her exactly what type of lady he desired and would only ever desire again. It was Noel. She was who he had searched for his entire life. The lady who fulfilled his every desire.

His thumb brushed across her bottom lip, and the tip of her tongue darted out in a responsive motion. Noel watched Ravencroft's gaze darken with an emotion more explosive than mere desire. His look held the state of how he wanted to possess her heart and soul. She never imagined in all of her silly romantic dreams of a passion so intense. Since Ravencroft had displayed nothing but a doting nature to her before this, Noel was unprepared for how to react. Would Ravencroft think her too wanton if she acted out her desires or would he finish what he had started the previous day?

As much as she wanted to give in to her desire, she needed to hear the rest of his explanation. If they were to have any chance of happiness, then she needed to trust him. At one time, she would have defended his character to anyone who spoke otherwise. However, her capture had left her in doubt, and until he confessed his secrets, she refused to give him her heart.

With reluctance, she pulled back and pushed herself off his lap. If she were to keep her wits about her, then she must put distance between them. Not that she had the space to roam very far. But sitting on his lap was a temptation she must not indulge in. Not right now, anyway.

Ravencroft groaned at her departure from his lap. He was mere seconds away from tasting her delectable lips. He sensed her eagerness, too. Her eyes were clouded with desire, declaring her every thought. She wanted him to make love to her, of that he was certain. However, he understood her reluctance, too.

He pulled out the letters in his suit coat and held them out. "These should answer your questions regarding your family."

Noel took the letters. "Thank you."

Ravencroft's gaze captured Noel. She saw how her withdrawal bothered him. She wished to ease his doubt, but it was impossible when she suffered from her own doubts. What caught her by surprise was the vulnerability in his eyes. It was then she realized Ravencroft was as much a victim in this situation as she was.

She took a step toward him. "Ravencroft?"

His lips tugged upward. "I thought we agreed on Gregory." He rose before she reached him. "I am stepping outdoors for a spell and will allow you privacy to read your letters."

Noel held her hand out to touch him as he passed, but he avoided her touch and walked outside. She frowned over his departure, unsure about his sudden change of mood. She sighed, settling on the sofa. The letters lay in her lap as she tried to piece together the shift in his emotions.

After some reflection, Noel realized it wasn't Ravencroft who kept changing moods. It was her. She lay in his arms, showing him how she longed for his kiss, and then she pulled away. When he opened himself up to her, it was she who kept distance between them. She was the fickle one in this relationship. But in her defense, the gentleman held no clue how he rattled her senses.

She held the letters up and noticed they were from Graham and Maggie. She would read Graham's letter first. Because it probably held the explanation she fretted over and a plan on how to proceed. Then she would read Maggie's letter, which was her sister's means of teasing her.

Hello Pipsqueak,

Or should I call you trouble? Now I expected this type of behavior from Maggie, perhaps even Eden, but certainly not from you. I didn't realize you felt neglected and in need of attention to get yourself kidnapped by the notorious Lady Langdale. If so, I would have teased you a bit more.

All humor aside, I hope you will forgive us for not coming to your rescue sooner. I will leave your fiancé to answer your questions about the delay. In his defense, if I were in his position, I would have reacted the same. Without knowing your location and the severity of Lady L's unpredictable behavior, Dracott and Ravencroft advised us to plan an escape where you would come to no harm. And to do so, you must remain under her control. But fear not, we shall have you home soon.

But then again, with the amount of teasing you are sure to receive, you might wish we never rescued you. Trousers? 'Tis so unlike you, my dear. I will warn you to prepare yourself because Maggie has made a list of teasing remarks for once you return home.

I hope this letter helps to reassure you. Chin up, my dear. You are a Worthington and you have the skills to survive someone as brutal as Lady Langdale. And if I can offer you a bit of advice? Go easy on the bloke. His actions to this point show proof of how he cares about you. While our brother would disagree, I believe Ravencroft is trustworthy and is worthy of your love. However you wish to proceed with the gentleman is entirely up to you. I will offer my support either way. But while you're in this predicament, trust him as I would.

Your devoted brother (and soon-to-be rescuer),

Graham

Noel folded the letter in her lap and stared at the door. Should she trust the man who stood outside? He was a contradiction to the gentleman who had courted her over the past year. Her common sense told her to follow her brother's advice, yet her heart urged her to keep up the walls of defense. That was the problem. She may appear like a lighthearted debutante without a care in the world. However, it was a façade she had perfected over the years to protect herself. The question she needed to answer was if she still wanted to protect herself from Ravencroft. Because of the situation they found themselves in, they either endured life's hardships together or worked separately to overcome this tribulation.

Sometimes walls were meant to be torn down.

Chapter Eleven

RAVENCROFT STOOD OUTSIDE THE cottage, surveying his surroundings. He started along the drive and saw how close to the road they were, a detail to use to their advantage if they escaped. However, the closer he drew, he saw Lady L had stationed two men on both sides of the drive. Their presence alone should draw curiosity in the countryside. Unless this was a road never traveled. His gaze scanned the horizon, and to his disappointment, there wasn't another home anywhere in the distance. Lady L had isolated them, and no one would question the reason for their presence at the cottage.

He turned back to the cottage and noted only one guard stood watch. Ravencroft didn't recognize any of the guards and assumed Lady L had recruited them after he left the organization. He needed to learn if he could bribe them or if they had pledged their loyalty to Lady L's cause. In the meantime, he needed to accustom himself to his surroundings, like Dracott had taught him years ago. Who knew a brief stint in crime would help him at a later date?

He motioned to the guard that he was stepping into the woods. "A moment of privacy, mate?"

The guard grunted his approval.

Ravencroft rounded the corner and realized why no one guarded behind the cottage. Nothing but a forest of trees surrounded it. Their only means of escape was past a guard who would prevent them from any attempt they made. He wouldn't risk Noel's safety. Not yet, anyway.

Ravencroft waited for a while before returning. Once he reached the guard, he needed to know where the guard's loyalty stood. At the very least, he needed to cause doubt with the guard in his position.

Ravencroft grimaced. "I hate to ask what you did to deserve this lowly position. Did you put sugar in her tea?"

The guard didn't reply, only snarled at him. Ravencroft hadn't taken in the guard's build before, but the snarl was menacing enough for him to notice the brute's strength. Ravencroft could hold his own and had spent many afternoons boxing at Gentleman Jack's, but even he realized his limitations. And the guard before him was one he wouldn't tangle with in a dark alley. The man's muscles bulged out of his shirt, and his thighs were as wide as wooden logs. He wished he had taken a better look at the other guards. Still, he continued to provoke a reaction.

He shrugged. "I only ask because she keeps her best men at her side and leaves these lowly jobs for the guards she doesn't trust."

His comment drew a frown from the guard, but still no reply.

Ravencroft folded his fingers over his palm and tilted them back and forth, examining them. "I would know. She never trusted me either and always assigned me to jobs like these. Stuck out in the middle of nowhere with men I never trusted." Ravencroft looked to the sky. "And the worst part, there is never any shelter during a storm. Not to mention the scraps she leaves for food." He ended with a shudder of the conditions he described.

Then the guard did the unexpected. He barked out a laugh. "She said you would attempt this ploy. Also alleged you were a weasel of an earl who imagined himself better than he was. Not so high and mighty now, are we, Mr. Aristocrat?"

Ravencroft bowed to him. "No. I do not suppose I am."

After taking pleasure from the guard's surprise, he went back inside. He chuckled at how he had gotten in the last barb. While the guard meant to attack his character, he only helped Ravencroft determine the guard's loyalties. After a few more interactions, he believed the guard would sway to their side.

With a newfound determination to help them escape, he was eager to share his findings with Noel. She still sat on the sofa, lost in her thoughts, staring at the letter in her lap. While he worried about what her siblings wrote to her about him, he also couldn't care less. His attitude gave him the courage to face his demons and allow no one to come between them. Caring siblings or not. It only mattered how Noel cared about him.

"I hope the letters helped," Ravencroft said.

Noel raised her eyes, focusing on Ravencroft. She hadn't realized he came back inside. "Yes. Well, at least Graham's letter." She raised the other letter. "I've yet to read Maggie's note."

"Do you want me to leave again?" He gestured toward the door.

"No. 'Tis unnecessary. I feel my sister's missive is only to torment me."

Ravencroft's brows drew together. "How so?"

"Graham so much as hinted at it in his letter. It seems my family has found humor in the attire I wore when I snuck out of the house. Their torment shall be endless upon my return."

Ravencroft almost made a comment about their insincerity, but the smile gracing Noel's face showed how she would endure their teasing with a friendly nature. Her family was a far cry different from his own. When he and Dracott gave each other a hard time, it was done with layers of sarcasm, but the Worthingtons always held mischief with their comments. Even Lady Worthington joined in occasionally with the teasing. If not, she always sat back, smiling at their antics, enjoying herself while her children found amusement at each other's expense.

Ravencroft shrugged instead. "Perhaps not read it and wait for the inevitable."

Noel laughed. "No. It is best if I read it now. So I can at least prepare a few comebacks of my own and be ready to surprise them."

Ravencroft lost himself in her laughter. The twinkling melody soothed his worried soul. Noel never ceased to amaze him with her ability to adapt to whatever circumstance she found herself in. Most ladies would remain in tears over their capture and the conditions forced upon them. But Noel sat before him, smiling without a worry at their predicament. He sensed it troubled her, but she didn't allow it to consume her.

He held out his hand. "Would you like me to read it instead?"

Noel beamed at him, holding out the letter. "That sounds splendid. That way, it will seem as if Maggie is teasing me herself. We may as well amuse ourselves for a bit before we return to our serious conversation."

Ravencroft cleared his throat before he began.

Dearest Noel,

Where shall I begin? I am shocked, and I mean shocked, at your choice of clothing. Breeches? Why, your display of indecency has brought shame upon our family name. A Worthington lady dressing like a boy will cause the tongues to wag and gossip unkindly.

Wherever did you find such clothing to wear? One would think you were a hoyden, gallivanting around in such attire.

Oh, I have more clever ones, but I prefer to tease you with those once you return. And you will, dear sister. Have faith in our brothers, Dracott, and Ravencroft. Out of all of us, you are the wisest when dealing with a crisis. Your ability to handle any situation with charm and wit will only work to your advantage.

Take care and we will rescue you soon. However, once you return, you will find yourself bombarded with so much teasing you will wish you remained captured.

Your devoted sister,

Maggie

Ravencroft tugged at his cravat. "Maggie only intended the letter for your eyes alone."

Noel waved her hand. "Nonsense. Maggie's only intention is to tease me."

"Umm. I do not believe so. Here." He thrust the note in her hands before striding to the kitchen area.

Noel watched Ravencroft digging through a picnic basket, pulling out food. He appeared uncomfortable with whatever Maggie had stated at the end of her letter. If she didn't know any better, she would think her sister's words flustered him. Which would explain the redness spreading across his cheeks. With curiosity, she lifted the letter to finish reading.

P.S.

As for Ravencroft, he withheld information about your disappearance because he believed himself capable of returning you safely home on his own. Once he realized how impossible it was, he told us everything. Graham and Crispin insisted he play along with Lady L's game because it was the only way to gather enough information on your location to make a rescue.

I shall be honest with you about how I never trusted Ravencroft throughout your engagement. I even asked Crispin to investigate him. Which now I realize was pointless since they are brothers. However, Crispin stands faithfully by Ravencroft's side and trusts him with his life. I guess I plead with you to do the same. I have set my misgivings to the side and I urge you to trust him, too.

At one time, you idolized Ravencroft. You thought him the most divine gentleman to have ever graced the earth. When you met him, some unknown fate drew you to each other. You saw in him what no one else ever did. Draw on that faith now. Open your heart to him and forgive him for his dishonesty and misplaced trust. Learn about what shaped him to be who he is today. Once you do, you shall never doubt his character ever again.

Just a little advice from your little sister.

We all love you, Noel. Return home to us safely.

Mags

Oh my. That was quite a postscript her sister had added. Who knew her sister held such a perception of another soul? Maggie's focus usually tended toward surrounding herself with nature while riding her horse. Now she wrote as a mature woman with life experience. Noel never held a clue about

Maggie's dislike for Ravencroft. Had he realized her sister disliked him? Another question to add to her long list.

The last paragraph of the letter held the most impact on Noel concerning the doubts she clung to about Ravencroft. Maggie wrote the truth when she described how Noel felt about Ravencroft. The first moment she laid eyes on him, her heart had declared he was the gentleman she would spend the rest of eternity with. Even as she stared at him now, that feeling never wavered. It might sway with uncertainty, but it remained the same. She couldn't imagine her life without him. Her need to learn about his past, his actions concerning her disappearance, and his plans for the future prompted her to his side.

"May I help?" Noel asked.

Ravencroft nodded toward the shelves hung on the wall. "You can gather the plates and utensils."

They worked quietly, setting the table for their meal. Once they sat down, Noel took over and filled their plates. Not once would Ravencroft meet her gaze. He still appeared embarrassed by her sister's words. She didn't understand why they bothered him, considering they were to his benefit.

"What meets us outside those doors?" Noel asked.

Ravencroft set his fork down. "Three men guard near the area. Two near the end of the drive and one by the cottage. Since I don't recognize them, they must be Lady L's new recruits. I tried to test the loyalty of the guard outside the door."

Noel's eyebrows lifted in doubt. "How did you fare?"

Ravencroft smirked. "The bloke was most insulting, but I surprised him with my response. I believe I can convince him to switch sides."

"Do you not mean *we* can convince him?"

While he didn't want Noel to interact with the guards, he needed to show her they worked together as a team. "Yes. *We.*"

Noel nodded, then continued eating. "What else did you learn of the surroundings?"

She cringed at her question, and guilt nibbled at her conscience for deceiving him about her knowledge of their whereabouts. She would admit the truth as soon as he confessed his secrets.

"Trees surround the cottage on all sides, and I don't see any other homes nearby. It isn't possible to escape through the trees and remain unscathed. Our only hope is to persuade the guard to switch sides."

Noel finished chewing on a bite of cheese. "We can always wait out Lady L and supply her with drawings of Reese's townhome."

Ravencroft growled. "I will not aid that witch in destroying anyone I care about any longer."

Noel didn't understand how Ravencroft's annoyance stirred emotions in her so strongly. She ached to have him unleash his passionate fire on her soul. To take her with abandonment, leaving her with no doubt of his affections. She wanted to provoke him into that very act, but she would wait. Now wasn't the time to explore her fantasies. She still needed him to confide in her.

"I understand. What if you draw a townhome similar to Reese's but with modifications?"

Ravencroft narrowed his gaze. "A set of false drawings?"

"Yes."

He leaned over and kissed Noel. "You are brilliant. I knew the day I met you how amazing you were."

Noel blushed. "You did?"

"Oh yes."

"How?"

Ravencroft frowned. "How?"

"Yes. How did you reach that conclusion?"

He leaned back in his chair, contemplating how to answer her question without offending her. "While you present yourself as a simpleminded debutante, boasting of catching the elusive Lord Ravencroft to your peers, I see it for what it is. An act for no one to notice your genuine kindness and intelligence. And why? Because I believe it protects anyone from getting too close and understanding how your mind works. You don't want any attention focused on your intelligence. You wish to enjoy people's kindness and believe in those who don't believe in themselves."

Ravencroft sat forward to finish his explanation. "You want to live a simple life with no drama. While you enjoy the attention, it is all a front. You interject yourself into situations to right a wrong or to defend someone less fortunate. Your wit always outsmarts your opponents. They do not realize who they confronted after you finish with them. Which only leaves me to wonder, am I one of your unfortunate souls you have rescued with your undying devotion?"

Noel toyed with her napkin. "You sound confident in how you regard me."

"Because I am. Never underestimate my affections where you are concerned."

Noel raised her gaze to his. "Then why have you never expressed your affection?"

Ravencroft sighed. "Because we fell into a routine I assumed you preferred, and I did not want to risk jeopardizing our relationship."

"Because of the financial wealth you would gain once we married?" Noel whispered.

He ran a hand through his hair in frustration at the turn of their conversation. He never wanted to touch on this subject with Noel. It showed a part of himself he wasn't proud of. He had hoped it would go unspoken and they would resume their relationship as before. But he should've known the passion they shared had changed their path's direction.

"Honestly?" At her nod, he answered her. "At first, yes, it was my primary reason. But then I grew to care for you after I became acquainted with your true nature, and my reasons changed. However, you showed no interest in me other than an object you favored on your arm to flaunt at the ton in your success at acquiring a groom. However, now I have learned differently of your affections, and my reasons have changed once again."

Noel's lips twisted. "To what?"

The smile Ravencroft bestowed on Noel left her in no doubt of what his reasons had changed to. The gesture was a cross between a rake set out to seduce an innocent lady and a gentleman who adored the lady before him. Once again, he stirred her emotions into a whirlwind of need. Even though she eagerly awaited his answer, once he uttered the words, there was no turning back for them. She either had to accept his reasons or end their relationship.

Noel's eyes glazed over with desire. While she pretended indifference to what he wished for, her body told a different story. She leaned toward him, eager to hear his response. Her tongue kept sliding out to lick across her bottom lip. He wondered what she would do if he picked her up and carried her to the bed in the corner. Would she object to his advances? Or would her soft sighs echo around the cottage while he ravished her lips, her luscious nipples poking through her shirt, the sweet nectar between her thighs? He longed to savor her sweetness again.

Ravencroft drew in a deep breath to bring himself under control. Her dreamy gaze had taken a hold of his senses. He must stop this line of questioning or else lose the last of his sanity.

Ravencroft started clearing the table. "To reasons I shall divulge at a more appropriate time. For now, we must rest. Tomorrow we can figure out how to get ourselves out of the mess we are in."

Noel stood. "But we have not finished our discussion on what led us to this predicament."

Ravencroft sighed. "I understand. May we continue tomorrow? I would like to give the guards the impression we have retired for the evening so I can spy on their movements."

"That sounds reasonable." She started toward the door.

"Where are you going?" Ravencroft barked.

Noel felt her cheeks warm. "I need to take care of my personal needs."

Ravencroft fought to calm himself. She scared him by attempting to walk outdoors. His fear for her safety would be his downfall if he didn't pull himself together. They had no privacy in this cottage, and once again, he failed to recognize her needs.

"Of course. Let me escort you outdoors."

Noel's cheeks grew redder. "I will be fine."

Ravencroft noticed her discomfort but feared for her safety around the guards. "Can we compromise and keep the door open?"

Noel nodded and rushed away before she grew any more embarrassed. The guard came to attention when she flew outside and she pointed to the woods, mortified to have to explain her situation to a complete stranger. It was dreadful enough she had to explain to Ravencroft. Which was her own fault. If she only trusted him enough to reveal the secret room Graham and Ralston had built in the cottage, she could've relieved herself in privacy. Now her fate led her to the woods. She hurried to the trees before the sun disappeared.

Once she finished her business, she strolled back to the cabin, noting nothing had changed since her last visit. Except the overgrowth of the trees near the road now hid the cottage.

She stopped near the guard. "Would you care for anything to eat?"

"No thank you, my lady. Lady L left us provisions," he informed her.

Noel offered him a smile in kindness and walked inside, closing the door behind her. She almost walked into Ravencroft because he stood right inside the cottage, awaiting her return. The frown on his face showed his displeasure at her talking to the guard. But he held himself back from reprimanding her. She had to give him credit because her brothers would have raged over her pleasant exchange with the guard.

Noel walked past him, smiling at his attempt to treat her as an equal. She continued to the bed and drew back the quilt. After tugging the drawstring loose on the breeches, they slid down her legs. She stepped out of them and bent over. If she wasn't mistaken, her action prompted a groan from Ravencroft. She wanted to peek to see if she was correct but didn't wish for him to realize her intention.

Noel may have pulled away from his kiss earlier, but she had no intention of pulling away again. She would follow Maggie's advice and forgive his past misdeeds. She needed no explanation because she loved him. Ravencroft was a lonely soul who had suffered through life's hardships without love. Noel wanted to wrap him in her warm embrace and ease his loneliness. She hoped to convince him of a future together.

Ravencroft groaned when Maggie bent over to retrieve her breeches from the floor. The shirt rode high, and he caught sight of her ass cheeks. It beckoned him to come closer and cup them in his hands while his fingers stroked her warm pussy. Why in the hell didn't she sleep in the damn breeches? Now he would spend his night tormented by fantasies he must not act upon. She may appear sweet and innocent, but after he had tasted her sweetness, Ravencroft believed her to be the devil's temptress sent to torment him with decadent thoughts. When she crawled on the bed and patted the spot next to her, he shook his head back and forth rapidly.

"You need your sleep, and I need to spy," Ravencroft reminded her.

Noel pouted. "But you need to sleep too."

Ravencroft stared out the window, fighting his urge to join her. "Later."

"Good night, Gregory," Noel whispered.

"Sleep well, Noel."

Ravencroft closed his eyes and pressed his forehead to the windowpane. When she whispered his name, it took everything he had not to join her. He didn't dare glance over his shoulder. Just the image of her alone, so close and lying on a bed, was enough to heighten his arousal. And when he fell asleep, it would be on the sofa or the floor. It would be an impossible feat to keep his hands to himself if he joined her on the bed.

Ravencroft blew out the candles and took up his watch at the window. She understood his reason for spying on the guards, but she also sensed it was an excuse to stay away from her. With the moon shining through the window, she took him in. He wore a pensive expression, and his shoulders hunched up with his tension. Did something else bother him besides her kidnapping?

Noel recalled their conversation and realized he had regarded her as a shallow lady at first, but over time, he had changed his opinion. Shame overcame her at how his statement rang true. She had paraded around on his arm, gloating her success at capturing his attention to the ton. But he was mistaken about her reason. The gossipmongers had whispered about his disappearance from society once he arrived on the scene. And every lady professed how they would capture him as a groom. So she understood why he assumed she had ensnared his attention to raise her standing amongst the ton.

When in fact it irritated her how the vipers talked about him behind his back but fell at his feet whenever he arrived at a function. While Ravencroft presented himself as a charming gentleman, she had noticed his insecurity and wanted to welcome his return with her friendship. She thought if she showed interest and he returned the attention, then the other ladies would search for another soul to sink their claws into. Noel never imagined he would propose. She supposed she enjoyed the attention of their engagement and how he continued to dote on her at every opportunity. After her friends found their happily ever after, she had dreamt of it for herself.

She had settled into their comfortable relationship and learned not to expect anything more than what they shared. Ravencroft was a safe choice, and they would lead a drama-free life. One much different from her childhood, where her father had belittled her mother at every opportunity and terrorized his children with his cruel behavior. Ravencroft had shown her he would provide her with a calm and secure marriage.

So when he asked for her hand in marriage, her pride had inflated at securing a successful match. And perhaps gloated more than she needed to. She had only wanted to show the vipers how much they never deserved him. She had never meant to demean him or their relationship.

Noel could argue how he had never shown any interest in anything more from their relationship. He charmed her family and friends and worshipped at her feet in front of the ton. But he never tried to get her alone. Ravencroft had led Noel to believe he wanted nothing more from their relationship than what they presented to everyone.

Because if he had, he would've stolen a kiss or two. Whisked her away to seduce her. Drew her hand in his while nobody noticed. Asked for a private walk through the garden. Whispered scandalous words in her ear. However, he had never made a single attempt at seduction.

Did he even wish to?

Chapter Twelve

RAVENCROFT RELAXED ONCE NOEL'S movement on the bed settled. Against his better judgment, he glanced over his shoulder. She had spread out across the bed with the pillow wrapped in her arms. He released a sigh. He'd been too harsh with her earlier when he discussed how she treated him throughout their courtship. But he didn't confess how honored it made him feel because he kept up a wall between them. She deserved someone better than him.

When he first pursued Noel, it had been because of her brother's influence. However, she had hooked him in her grasp with her sharp wit and the kindness she bestowed on others after a few visits. Her enthusiasm for the simplest of pleasures gave him hope of a peaceful life they would share. Noel would never expect much from him or cause him any drama.

But with each event he escorted her to, she kept nestling her way into his heart. He had become enamored with her beauty, and every evening when he escorted her home, he resisted her. He wished for them to speak their vows before he staked his needs. However, his resistance had fallen after she appeared at his home, making demands in her irresistible attire.

Ravencroft watched the guards follow the same routine from when he worked for Lady Langdale. He needed his rest to stay alert tomorrow. However, Noel drew him toward her. He wandered to the bed, promising himself he only wanted to check if she slept well and nothing more. Except when he gazed down upon her, he realized he stood above her for his own selfish reasons. He wanted to slide under the covers, pull her into his arms, and ravish every delectable inch of her body.

He balled his hands into fists, fighting the temptation. With reluctance, he turned toward the sofa but stopped when Noel whimpered. He paused, turning back when her whimpers grew louder and she thrashed around on the bed.

"Gregory," Noel whimpered. "Help me."

His heart raced at the helplessness in her voice. It was his fault she suffered through a nightmare. He knelt on the bed. "Shh, Noel."

Instead of his words calming her, her arms swung out and she released a bloodcurdling scream. It sent shivers down his spine and reminded him of the terrors Dracott endured. He gathered her in his arms, shushing her and rubbing her back in a calming motion. Her breath hitched at his touch, and soon her breathing calmed. However, her hands still clutched at his shirt with distress. He settled his hand over one of them, peeled it away, and lifted it to his mouth. He placed soft kisses across her knuckles until her hand relaxed.

"Gregory," Noel whispered.

"Shh, love."

"What happened?"

"You had a nightmare. Try to go back to sleep. I'll keep you safe," Ravencroft murmured.

"Will you talk to me until I fall asleep?"

"About what?"

"Tell me about your estate." Noel snuggled into his arms.

Ravencroft clenched his eyes shut as her soft curves nestled into him. The vulnerability of the situation played havoc on his senses. While he wanted to comfort her and provide a sense of security, he really wanted to strip the shirt from her body and kiss all her worries away. He kept trying to remind himself that he was a gentleman, regardless of his scandalous thoughts.

"There isn't much to tell, other than my neglect."

Noel toyed with his buttons, wanting to undo them. "Do you hold any special memories of the place?"

Ravencroft smiled into the darkness as he thought of his childhood home. "Yes. I only hold cherished memories of my home. My father allowed me free rein over the estate in my youth and taught me how to love the land. I hope to give my children the same gift."

"Did your feelings ever change about your home after your mother left?" Noel questioned. Her curiosity prompted her to ask because after her father passed away, her home life had changed for the better.

Ravencroft slid his hand through her hair, enjoying how the softness caressed him. "Yes. For a while, I only felt relief because her selfishness made my father miserable. He catered to her every whim. However, nothing was ever to her satisfaction. For a short time, I despised the place because his wife's betrayal had broken my father's heart and he stopped caring. No matter what I tried, he never returned to the man I admired. When he grew ill, he begged for my forgiveness for failing to provide a stable home. Then, before he died, he pleaded with me to make him a promise I wanted to refuse. However, I could never refuse my father anything."

Noel had unbuttoned his shirt, and her hand slid against his warm chest. "What was the promise?"

His breath hitched at her touch. "To find my mother and forgive her. He told me I must because I had a brother who needed my help. My father learned the child's father had died and about the trouble my mother had entangled her and the child in. He wanted me to save my brother and bring him to our home."

Noel pressed her lips against his heart before laying her cheek on it. "And you fulfilled your father's promise."

"No. I only promised him so he could pass away in peace. Until my dying day, I will never forgive that woman for abandoning us and raising Dracott in hell. The promise will forever go unfulfilled," Ravencroft swore.

Ravencroft took a deep breath. Instead of calming Noel back to sleep, he told her a story filled with bitterness and strife. When she didn't respond, he thought she might have fallen back asleep or thought harshly of him.

Then her soft voice filled the cottage with her own heartache. "I hated my father and found joy when he died. Does that make me a horrible person?"

His arms squeezed around her. "No, my love. It only shows the depth of your emotions toward someone who caused you pain. You hold the freedom to express your own feelings about others. And no one holds the right to tell you differently."

"I never told another soul that before."

Ravencroft kissed the top of her head. "I will carry your secret to the grave and beyond."

She kissed his heart again before rolling on top of him. "You, my lord, must work on your bedtime stories. They are most depressing and will give our children nightmares."

Gregory stilled at her comment. When he noticed the smirk around her lips and how her eyes crinkled in amusement, he reacted with his heart's urgings. His hand curved around her cheek as he pressed his lips against hers. He wanted to steal her smile with his kiss. His tongue licked the upward slope of her lips. Noel's soft sigh urged him to deepen the kiss. Gregory slid his hands into her tresses, while his tongue dived inside and slid against hers.

Noel only meant to tease him with her comment to help lighten the mood. She never expected him to ravish her like a man starving for a taste of her lips. He never so much as responded when she undid his shirt and kissed his chest. But she learned he held himself back, when she only wanted him to kiss her senseless. She no longer desired the perfect gentleman; she desired a man who took what he wanted. She wanted him to succumb to their desires. Because Noel needed Gregory more than she needed to breathe.

Her hands trailed down his chest and wrapped around his waist, her fingers digging into his back as he claimed her as his. She wanted to wrap herself around him and absorb his heat. His security. His love.

Noel set his body aflame with her touch. He grew hotter with each caress of her nimble fingers. He rolled them over and pulled his lips away. When she whimpered, he smiled with amusement. "Our children?"

Noel pulled his shirt up to slide over his head. "Well, yes, Lord Ravencroft. How else will you fulfill your dream if we do not have any?"

He pressed his forehead against hers. "Noel, we must stop."

"Why?" she asked, sliding her hands over his chest and down to his stomach. Her fingers slid inside the waistband of his trousers.

He had no reasonable explanation for her other than her innocence and how he must act like a gentleman and protect her virtue. But his excuse only sounded weak to him and it would to Noel, too. When her fingers dipped lower, he sucked in his breath. For an innocent, she learned quickly.

Noel wanted to chuckle at Ravencroft's indecision when he only had himself to blame. If he hadn't awakened her desires, she never would have known the pleasure of his touch. It would appear he needed a little more persuasion.

She slid her leg up and wrapped it around his waist, pressing against him intimately. His hardness pressed into her core, heightening her need for Gregory to pleasure her.

"I do not see any reason why we must stop." Her lips kissed a path along his neck. "We are alone." Her teeth tugged at his earlobe. "And I am most eager for you to teach me the propositions you made the other evening."

Gregory pulled her hands off him and held them above her head. Each breath he drew in reflected how his resistance crumbled. The desire in her gaze pulled at him to fall and worry about the circumstances later. When her leg slid up and down his, and her tongue struck out to lick her lips, it was his downfall.

He tightened his grip on her wrists, which only earned him a moan of pleasure. "You have no clue what you have awakened."

Her smile was seduction itself. "Perhaps not, but I am excited to learn."

His other arm wrapped around her waist and lifted her against his chest. "After this, I will no longer be your meek fiancé who you pet in affection."

"If I wanted a pet, I would have one," Noel purred. "I want you."

"You are foolish, but I am powerless to resist you. You are a temptress the devil sent to distract me."

Noel leaned forward to steal a kiss, but Ravencroft pulled away. "Distract you from what?"

"From redeeming myself," Gregory whispered before devouring her lips with one passionate kiss after another, leaving her no time to ask for an explanation. His kisses were relentless as they heightened her desire to where she was powerless to respond.

"Do not fight it, temptress, let it wash over you," Gregory demanded.

Gregory's hand skated up her shirt and cupped her breast, teasing her nipple with a soft pinch. His exquisite torture was far from over. His hand trailed down her stomach and sank into her curls, drawing forth a moan filled with a need only he could satisfy. Her body came alive with every touch he bestowed on her.

"Tell me to stop, Noel," Gregory begged.

"Never," Noel promised.

Gregory growled, releasing her hands and stripping her bare. His eyes raked her in a breathtaking perusal, lingering on every curve and dip. His hands drew her legs apart, and his gaze fastened on her cunny. The darkness couldn't hide her desire from him. Her scent filled the air, drawing him deeper into her web.

"I warned you," Ravencroft declared before he slid between her legs and dragged his tongue against her core.

Noel gasped at his boldness. He gave her no gentle caress to warn her of his intentions but seized what he desired, leaving her moaning from the sinful delight his tongue ignited with each stroke. When he slid two fingers inside her, increasing her pleasure, she stood on the edge of a cliff, ready to fall. Then his touch softened, and his tongue gently caressed her folds, pulling her back.

Noel moaned. "Oh, Gregory."

Her whispered exclamation struck a return of his relentless attack on her senses. His fingers stroked in and out faster as his tongue flicked back and forth in rapid succession, pushing her back to the edge. She grasped his hair as she floundered and held him to her core.

Gregory was a drowning soul and never wanted to resurface from between her thighs. Noel's silky skin squeezed his head while his mouth plundered her divine sweetness. When she clutched his head to hold him, his cock demanded its release. But his torment had only just begun. He had warned her. The months he pretended his indifference because he didn't wish to frighten Noel with his passion unraveled with her promise of *never*.

His tongue slowed again, and he nipped at her pussy. Her soft whimpers were a melody that soothed his soul. However, when he possessed her body, he wanted to hear her beg him for release. When her thighs relaxed, he started his seduction again, only this time he wanted to taste her explosion and wouldn't relent until she did.

The push and pull of Gregory's seduction strung out Noel's desire. Her body willingly surrendered to each caress and kiss. When he struck out again, his seduction increased with each caress of his tongue. Noel hurtled over the cliff and soared to his demands.

Noel shook against him as she exploded on his tongue. He kissed the inside of her thighs, working his way up her body to settle between her breasts. His hand stroked her, continuing her journey to a fever pitch, while he drew her nipples between his lips. While he sucked on the sweet buds, his tongue swirled around, savoring her delicious nectar.

A haze surrounded Noel, one she never wanted to return from. She never knew heaven would feel so incredible. Gregory had warned her, but she had thought he meant to convince her to stop. However, he made true to his threat.

Gregory hovered over Noel, noting the dazed expression in her eyes. "Do you still hold curiosity about my propositions?"

Gregory gave her one last chance to stop him before he went any further.

Noel laced her fingers behind his neck, drawing his head lower. "Yes. However, you seem a bit overdressed."

Before he could protest, Noel kissed him. A long, slow kiss to show him she very much wanted him to continue making love to her. Her tongue traced his lips, darting in to touch his tongue before darting back out. He craved to kiss her for an eternity each time she teased him with her kisses. When her tongue glided against his, he took over the kiss.

Noel moaned her pleasure over Gregory's possession. He abandoned his doubt with each kiss. Her hand skated along his back to reach his trousers, trailing her fingers around to the front. She encountered his hardness pressing through his pants. Noel rested her hand against him and touched his desire.

"Yes, most definitely overdressed," she murmured.

Noel's touch through his clothing almost caused him to spend himself. He couldn't blame his two years of celibacy as an excuse for his lack of control. It was the temptress who teased his senses that unraveled him. Her fingers tugged at the placket of his trousers. He must take control again before she wrapped her soft hand around his cock. One touch and he would embarrass them both.

He tugged her hands back up above her head. Instead of lying still as she did before, she twisted her hands back and forth, fighting against his hold.

Noel pouted. "No fair. I wish to touch you in the same manner you touched me. Was that not part of your proposition?"

Gregory moaned at how the very act would feel. He imagined nothing more pleasurable than her pouty lips wrapping around his cock and sucking him off. He tore at the buttons keeping him confined and kicked his trousers away. His other hand gripped his cock, trying to ease the ache consuming him. However, his need only intensified as he slid his gaze along Noel's curves. Her rosy nipples hardened at his perusal, and the dew of her desire wet her curls. If he were a betting man, he would say he would sink into her cunny with one easy glide. But he changed his mind and ached for her touch before he did so. He was a glutton for punishment and wondered if his imagination would ring true.

Noel shivered at Gregory's devilish smile. Not from fear, but from what he would teach her. He released her wrists and drew one of her hands down the length of his body before settling on his hardness.

"Far be it for me not to be fair," Gregory growled.

He didn't need to wonder any longer. Noel's touch far surpassed anything he had ever imagined. Her sensuous touch as it stroked his cock was a cross between a crushing ache that begged for release and hoped the wondrous sensation lasted for hours on end.

"Can I kiss you here?" Noel asked. Her thumb brushed back and forth across the tip of his cock.

She asked her question with such innocence, but the act itself held a decadence he craved from her. When she lifted her hand and slid her thumb into her mouth, sucking off his wetness, Gregory lost what remained of his control.

He glided his cock between her folds. Her wetness helped to ease his cock inside her in one smooth glide, just as he thought. When he met the wall to take her virginity, he paused, staring into Noel's eyes.

Noel lost herself in the need shining from Gregory's eyes. Even though he held himself back from sliding deep inside her, his gaze conflicted with his actions. When she pressed her hips up, pushing past the barrier of her innocence, his eyes darkened and his need grew fiercer. If that was even possible. She soon learned how intense his need for her was.

His hand guided her leg up higher against his hip as he slid in and out of her in a slow rhythm. Each time he slid in deeper than the last, drawing out her moans and capturing them with his kisses. Noel arched her body into his with each thrust. Her nipples tingled each time they scraped against his chest. Her body became inflamed as her soul left her to join with his on this breathtaking journey of becoming one.

The walls he had built around his heart crumbled stone by stone with every stroke inside Noel. Never had he experienced a connection with another so powerful. His hands wandered her body with a desperate need to touch her. His mouth stayed fastened to hers, absorbing every one of her deep moans into his soul.

Noel's body moved in perfect rhythm with his. Each time he pressed in deeper, she rotated her hips. Their bodies fit together perfectly, and Noel was a natural in the art of lovemaking. Her body responded to his every demand. Her pussy tightened around his throbbing cock. He wanted to join her as she exploded around him. No. He needed to join her.

"Gregory, please!" Noel whimpered.

Noel didn't know if she pleaded or demanded for Gregory to lose control and send them spiraling over that cliff together. She dangled on the edge again, and she wanted Gregory to join her.

Gregory drew Noel into a deep kiss as he sent them over the edge, swallowing her screams of pleasure. He drew her into his embrace, their bodies trembling from the turbulent storm of their passion. He closed his eyes, enjoying the comfort of holding her so close to his heart, and prayed Noel wouldn't regret their lovemaking in the morning.

Gregory's body relaxed under her, and Noel realized he had fallen asleep. She tilted her head back and observed him from between her lashes. His face had softened from the frown he had worn all day. He carried a heavier burden than she had imagined. She hoped when he awakened, he didn't consider their lovemaking another burden he had to carry. But one he wanted to.

Their lovemaking wasn't a mistake. It was a beacon to their future.

Chapter Thirteen

NOEL STRETCHED, HER BODY tender in a few spots. A smile lifted her cheeks as the memories of their lovemaking came rushing back. She rolled over, reaching for Gregory, but found an empty spot next to her instead. Her gaze searched the cottage, and she found him sitting at the table in deep concentration, scribbling on the paper Lady L had left. A lock of his hair hung over his eyes and he kept swiping at it while he worked.

To her delight, he had only drawn on his trousers and left his shirt off. Noel's fingers itched to caress the expanse of his muscular back. She wondered what particular activity he partook in to maintain such a fine form. Her body grew warm as she remembered the strength of his legs entwined with hers while they made love. Ravencroft disheveled was indeed a splendid sight to admire. As she informed anyone who would listen, he was most *divine*.

Ravencroft sensed the moment Noel had awakened. He tried to focus on the drawings. But his desire to crawl under the covers and love her again demanded for him to give in. Holding her in his arms when he woke up this morning was the most amazing gift he had ever received. He waited for her to declare how they had made a mistake last night

However, the soft sighs she made when aroused floated across the cottage, washing over him.

His pencil snapped in two from his brutal hold. "Good morning, Noel."

He had to acknowledge she had awakened, hoping to prompt her to rise for the day. Because once again, his control slipped from his grasp. He had warned her, but he hadn't taken his own warning seriously. In his defense, he hadn't realized the force of their attraction would blow his world apart.

When he heard Noel's dejected sigh, he chuckled. At least he wasn't alone with how he wished the morning could proceed. But Lady L would arrive soon, and he needed hours on end to worship Noel's body and slack his desires. Also, Lady L must never learn of their intimacy. It wouldn't bode well for Noel. He would risk everything to protect Noel from Lady L's wrath, even deny making love to her.

Gregory made it clear with his greeting and how he continued working that he expected her to rise from the bed and start her day. She grabbed his shirt hanging on the bedpost and slipped it over her head. It hung past her knees, but the silk caressed her skin instead of making her itch from the rough fabric of the shirt she had stolen from Maggie.

She brought the material to her nose and inhaled Gregory's scent. The musky sandalwood, mixed with his own unique aroma, brought a flood of desire to her core. It would appear after one night of passion, scandalous thoughts ruled her mind.

Noel sauntered over to Gregory and leaned over his shoulder. "What has demanded your attention from my warm embrace?"

Ravencroft laughed at her bold question. "Have I created a wanton temptress after showing her the pleasure of my propositions?"

"Mmm, answering a question with a question, are we? Well, in that case . . ." She slid onto his lap. "Do you not have more propositions you wished fulfilled?"

Noel's arse nestled against his cock, and each time she shifted, his plan for the morning disappeared. The wicked act of her riding his cock consumed his thoughts. His hand slid under his shirt and sank into her folds. Noel's cunny was on fire and soaking wet. She moaned, pressing soft kisses to his chest. His thumb brushed against her clit as he sank a finger deep inside her pussy. They hadn't even shared a proper kiss good morning, and her body was already eager for him.

With her eyes heavy with desire, she looked like a package of sin wearing his shirt. Her nipples peaked through the opening, tempting him to throw her on the table and devour her. But his hunger to claim her demanded that he take her now.

"You are a damn temptation I do not have time for this morning, Miss Worthington," Ravencroft growled.

"Then make time, Lord Ravencroft." Noel moaned when his finger twisted inside her.

He swung her legs so that she straddled him. Then he opened his pants and pulled out his cock. "So you want to learn more about my propositions, do you?"

Noel nodded, biting her bottom lip as she gazed upon Gregory's hand wrapped around his hardness. Before she could question him further, he lifted her and slid inside her warmth. Her eyes lowered at the scandalous pleasure from this position.

"Open your eyes, love," Gregory demanded.

"I thought . . ." Noel's tongue darted out to wet her lips.

"I cannot handle the sweet torture of your lips sucking the juices off my cock." His lips moved to her ear. "I would not last a minute before I flooded your mouth with my desire. No. We will have to wait for you to fulfill that proposition later."

Noel blushed at the debauchery of the act he described. Yet the words stroked the fire, consuming her. She moved her hips to ease the ache in her core. The throbbing strength of Gregory moved deeper inside her.

Gregory moaned. "That's it, love, ride my cock like the temptress you are."

He gripped her hips, guiding her on how to move. Her every movement hypnotized him under her spell. From the arch of her neck as she threw her head back to how her fingers gripped his shoulders as she slowly slid up and down. Each time she lowered back down, her confidence grew. Her body staked her demands, and he responded by shifting his hips upward, driving inside her deeply.

He tore his shirt off her and lowered his head to suck on her breasts. His teeth scraped across her nipple, earning him a rush of wetness. He sucked on the nipple harder until Noel grabbed his head and moved him to her other breast. Their bodies loved one another with wild abandonment.

Every stroke sent shock waves throughout her body. She wanted to wrap herself around Gregory and crawl inside him. Noel craved his touch on every part of her body. She needed his lips to caress her shattered soul. However, no matter where he kissed or touched, it wasn't enough. She only wanted more.

When Noel picked up the pace, Gregory sensed she was ready to fall apart in his arms. His hand lowered and stroked her, intensifying the pleasure when she pulled away. He kissed her as the passion ruling their bodies sent them flying over the edge in each other's arms.

Gregory's kiss turned gentle as Noel collapsed against him. He wrapped his arms around her and held her tightly. This lady would be the death of him if their passion continued to consume them. He thought last night held such an intensity because it was the first time they had made love. But today's

lovemaking proved his theory wrong. Now that he had
claimed her, Noel became a distraction he must overcome if
he wanted them to escape unharmed. He must resist her, no
matter how difficult it may be.

He stood up with her in his arms and carried her to the sofa.
After he laid her down, he covered her with a blanket. She
smiled up at him with a drowsy expression, and he placed a
kiss on her head. Then he returned to the table and pulled
on his shirt after fixing his trousers. As he buttoned his shirt,
he couldn't keep his gaze off her. Noel brought out every
protective instinct he held. He must find a way for them to
escape soon.

Gregory dipped a towel into the water and returned to her
side, pulling the blanket away. As gently as he could, he ran the
towel between her legs. When she winced, he felt like a brute
for taking her so soon. But when her fingers touched his face,
smoothing away his frown, he realized she didn't regret their
lovemaking. He wished he could draw her a bath and pamper
her with bubbles and perfumed soap.

Noel lay relaxed as Gregory cared for her. His gentle touch
made her feel special. While he had yet to answer every
question, she no longer doubted him. Instead, she trusted him
with her life. He deserved her honesty since he had offered
his. She would confess about the cottage after she got dressed
and ate breakfast.

He drew Noel's shirt over her head. "The reason I never
attempted to fight for your release was because I have
witnessed what happens when someone tries to escape from
Lady L's hold. I did not want to risk your life for my selfish
motives. While it broke me to leave you there, you were safer
under her control than if I fought for your freedom. Because
if they took me prisoner too, I could never have gotten help."

Noel buttoned the shirt and rose to finish dressing. "But are you not a prisoner now?"

Ravencroft nodded. "Yes. But Kincaid's men were tracking my every move. They would've passed the information about our location to our brothers. They will attempt a rescue soon. Also, I gave Dracott clues leading to Lady L's hideout. If for some reason Kincaid's men couldn't follow us, Dracott will track down Lady Langdale. In the meantime, we must form a plan of escape."

"How have our circumstances changed?"

Ravencroft stared out the window at the guards. "Because there are only three of them, and I believe we can outsmart them."

"How?"

His eyes squinted as he looked up the drive. A carriage rolled to a stop by the cottage. "I will explain later. Hurry and make the bed. Do not give any indication of our intimacy."

Noel wanted to question his order, but he sat back down at the table, returning to his drawings. "Gregory?"

Instead of answering her, he pointed to the bed. "Now, Noel."

She went from feeling loved to feeling like a filthy secret he wanted to keep from his lover. Had he lied to her about his connection to Lady Langdale? She drifted toward the bed, but before she pulled the quilt over the mattress, the door flew open and Gregory's mother sauntered inside. When she saw Noel, she appeared shocked with outrage.

"Why, you little harlot. How dare you ruin my Gregory's reputation as an upstanding gentleman with your scandalous seduction! I heard rumors of your sister-in-law seducing your brother. Is she responsible for teaching you how to trap a lord?" Lady Ravencroft accused.

Noel gasped, dropping the blanket and backing away from the bed. Lady Ravencroft's accusation left her speechless.

But the horror of the situation only increased when Lady L followed Gregory's mother inside, wearing a smirk at what she saw.

"Mother! That is enough!" Ravencroft roared.

He stormed across the cottage and stood in front of Noel, protecting her. But Noel refused to cower in front of these ladies. She stepped from behind him and finished making the bed, ignoring them. She refused to waste her breath defending herself from individuals who didn't deserve an explanation about their relationship. Gregory had already stated how she could ignore his mother. It was the perfect opportunity for her to show Lady Ravencroft that she cared little what the woman thought of her.

Lady L lifted the drawings off the table. "I see you took my advice to seduce the chit to get the information we needed."

Ravencroft looked at Noel with a guilty expression before moving toward the table. "I started the drawings this morning." He leaned close to whisper where only Lady L heard. "I shall finish by the end of the week."

Lady L studied him with a shrewd expression and then focused on Noel. She must have found satisfaction with their behavior because she turned on her heels to leave. When she reached the door, she paused. "I am sure you will, Lord Ravencroft. It appears the lady has fallen for your charm like all the others before. I shall allow your mother to share with you the change in our plans. I will return in three days for the final drawings. Try not to spend every minute between her thighs. You have work to finish."

Ravencroft gritted his teeth at her crudity and the false impression she gave Noel about his involvement with her plans. He wanted to defend himself, but he couldn't afford to have her impression change from how she presumed he tricked Noel. It was in their best interest if she left believing he had seduced Noel for the information he needed. Now he must deal with his mother. He only hoped Noel understood how he acted to fool them.

"Speak, Mother, then leave," Ravencroft demanded.

Lady Ravencroft tilted her chin, offended by her son's harsh tone. "I have persuaded Lady L to offer you a new condition for your help. Upon your release, you will show your gratitude by welcoming me back in your good graces."

"And why should I offer you any gratitude?"

Lady Ravencroft clutched her chest. "Because I discovered Lady Langdale had kidnapped you and your lovely fiancée and I went to the authorities with information on your location."

Noel moved to sit on the sofa, folding her hands in her lap as if she were only making pleasant conversation. "Very clever, Lady Ravencroft. You shine as a martyr, forcing Ravencroft to declare his forgiveness for your desertion, all the while sabotaging his well-standing name with your nefarious plot to ruin my family. However, I am curious about one matter. I know of Lady Langdale's reason for revenge against my brother, but what is yours?"

Ravencroft closed his eyes and blew out a breath. He had asked her to stay silent, but of course she refused to abide by his demand. At least she hadn't spoken a word around Lady Langdale. He opened his eyes to find Noel staring his mother down, waiting for a reply. His mother glared at Noel as she attempted to find an insult to put Noel in her place. However, with another glance at Noel, he realized he had underestimated her again. She didn't need his protection. She possessed enough confidence to handle his mother all on her own. Perhaps even Lady Langdale, too.

While wanting to play the hero by protecting her, he had failed to notice her strengths. Noel always came to the aid of others and defended the unfortunate. She had more than enough skills to defend herself. He leaned against the wall, waiting for his mother to answer. Noel could handle the situation. However, he wasn't a fool. Noel would unleash her fury at him for his callous treatment once his mother left.

"You are an impotent miss, are you not?" Lady Ravencroft snarled.

Noel responded by raising her eyebrow.

Lady Ravencroft turned toward her son. "Do you allow her to speak to me in that regard?"

Ravencroft held out his hands. "I am not in control of how Noel wishes to speak."

Lady Ravencroft humphed. "I hope after you speak your marital vows, you put a stop to her insolence."

He smiled at Noel. "Now why would I attempt such an act? I quite like her *insolence*."

"You act the same as your father. That man never had a backbone, either."

Ravencroft bowed. "Thank you for the compliment, Mother. I greatly admired my father. Except for how he devoted himself to you. In that I never understood. Now, if you will please answer Noel's question and be on your way."

Lady Ravencroft stalked toward the door. "Ask your mother, Lady Noel. She will know why I seek my revenge against the Worthington family. Let me say, as Ravencroft is like his father, your brother differs little from his."

Lady Ravencroft stormed away after delivering her cryptic comment. Ravencroft closed the door and moved to the window to watch their departure. Lady L had only left two guards behind, which meant she trusted the progress he had made. Or else it was a trap to catch him off guard to attempt an escape.

He waited for Noel's anger, but only silence filled the cottage. When he turned, he found Noel's gaze narrowed at him. She sat all prim and proper on the sofa as if they entertained guests, a contrast to the state of her clothing and the setting they were in. He took a step closer and noticed her disappointment.

Ravencroft placed his hands on the back of a chair. "Unleash your fury, my lady. I deserve every word."

Noel sighed. "Another aspect of my character you have no clue about. I am not one who allows her temper to rule her actions. Now Maggie, she is the spitfire of our family who will unleash her fury if wronged." Noel blew out a breath. "Eden is the most brutal. For if you anger her, she will take a bite out of you. As for Reese and Graham, they act as all men do. They are hotheaded and believe they are always correct. As for me, I prefer to understand a person's actions before responding myself. You are aware of what has upset me. Now I am allowing you to explain your actions before I make my decision on how to react. At the moment, I only hold disappointment in the way you handled Lady Langdale. As for your mother, I thank you for allowing me my voice when dealing with her."

Ravencroft moved around to sit in the chair. "My apologies. It seems I still have much to learn about your character. While protecting myself through our courtship, I did you a great injustice by not learning every facet of your personality. I stated yesterday how you may speak your mind to my mother whenever you need to. You have my respect for not allowing her to undermine you."

Noel pinched her lips, not satisfied with how he answered. "None of your explanation held the reason on why you acted as you did around Lady Langdale."

Ravencroft leaned forward. "I apologize for her disrespect. I needed her to believe how I charmed you into revealing the layout of your home. She needs to believe my intention to double-cross your family."

"Why?"

"So she would loosen the reins on the guards. When Lady L is confident her plan is succeeding, she errors in her judgements, making slight mistakes one can take advantage of. I, by no means, meant to tarnish what we have shared. I asked you to stay silent because I needed Lady L to believe I controlled your actions. While you are a strong independent lady who can handle herself, I still want to protect you in any way I can. Even from the vileness of others," Ravencroft explained.

Noel nodded. "Then she believes I am this meek lady who cannot defend myself, expecting nothing more from me because I am not a threat to her."

"Exactly. So when you strike, she will least expect it."

Noel's mouth lifted in a grin. "I forgive you."

"I do not deserve you."

Her smile turned impish. "Not yet. However, if you continue striving, I believe you will soon."

Ravencroft chuckled. "You are definitely a temptress sent by the devil to torment me."

Noel gasped, clutching at her chest. "To torment?"

He rose and leaned over to kiss her. "Yes, with your kindness. Sweetness. Forgiveness. And hopefully with your love."

"Mmm," Noel murmured into the kiss.

He didn't need to hope. Noel already loved Gregory.

Only she wasn't ready to tell him quite yet.

Chapter Fourteen

NOEL JOINED RAVENCROFT AT the table as she watched him draw out sketches of her home. She frowned over a mistake and pulled the drawing closer. In fact, not a single room matched those in Reese's townhome.

She pointed at the mistake. "You have drawn this room incorrectly."

Ravencroft continued sketching. "Yes, I have. I am taking your advice and making fake drawings."

Noel's brows crinkled. "But won't Lady L know you gave her false drawings?"

Ravencroft lifted his head. "How would she?"

"Because, you know." Her hand fluttered in the air to hide her discomfort at talking about such a delicate subject.

"No. Please enlighten me."

"She was Reese's mistress," Noel hissed.

Ravencroft chuckled, leaning back in the chair. "Yes, she was."

He should've elaborated on why Lady L would have no clue about Reese's townhome. However, Noel's behavior amused him, and he wanted to tease her.

Noel nodded at the drawings. "I am sure she will recognize you drew the layout wrong."

Ravencroft's lips twitched, holding back his laughter. "No, she will not."

Noel stood, placing her hands on her hips. "You underestimate a lady's memory. Believe me, she will know."

"First of all, she is no lady. And second, believe me, she has never stepped foot in your brother's townhome."

"But she was his mistress" Noel repeated.

"Noel, a gentleman never allows his mistress access to his home. He either visits her at her home or owns a house where they meet."

"They don't?"

"No."

"Why?" Noel asked.

Ravencroft sighed. "Because even an unmarried gentleman keeps his mistress a secret from his family. They are two different worlds that rarely ever cross. In some cases they do, but most gentlemen prefer they don't. Barbara Langdale would've only learned the layout of the townhome if she became Lady Worthington. That is why she will no remember or recognize we are providing her with false drawings."

"Oh." Noel bit at her bottom lip, debating if she should ask her next question. Never one to shy away from delicate topics she felt she had the right to ask. "Where do you visit your mistress?"

Noel's question caused him to break another pencil. "I have never had a mistress, nor do I ever plan on acquiring one."

Noel scoffed. "Please."

Ravencroft arched an eyebrow in question.

"You claim you never kept a mistress, yet how did you become skilled in the bedroom?"

"I never said I was a virgin. Nor have I denied the countless women I have bedded. I only state that I've never kept a mistress," Ravencroft drawled.

"Oh." Why was she incapable of saying anything witty to his comments this morning? Perhaps it was her lack of knowledge of how a gentleman caroused. One more question and she must finish for her peace of mind. And heart. She hated to hear of him with any other lady. "Since we are now intimate, will you cease with your other dalliances?"

Ravencroft sighed. "I haven't bedded another lady for over two years."

Noel's mouth hung open in shock. "Two years?"

"Yes. You will not hear a word of gossip about my involvement with another woman since your brother announced our engagement because there has been no one."

"May I ask why?" All right, she couldn't stop with the questions. Her mother always said her curiosity would get the best of her.

"Because I disliked the man I had become. I wanted to redeem myself into the man I deserved to be. I spent the past few years involved in Lady L's schemes and sullied my reputation," Ravencroft explained.

"Is that what Lady L meant earlier when she commented on you charming a lady to spill her secrets?" Noel asked.

Ravencroft ran his hand down his face. "Yes. Lady L would scout out a widow or lonely wife who was ripe for seduction. Then my job was to charm my way into their bed. Since a lonely wife didn't wish for her husband to learn of her affair, she would send the servants away, and a widow who didn't wish shame upon her name would do the same. Then while I seduced them abovestairs, Lady L's crew would ransack belowstairs for any valuables. Then we would leave town and move on to the next victim."

He looked at Noel after his explanation and saw her look of disappointment. It was the last of his secrets to share with her. The other secrets he held weren't his own to confess. He had made a promise to Dracott to keep the most valuable secret between them. And he wouldn't betray his brother as much as he wished to tell Noel because it placed the person's life at significant risk.

"That is the last of my morbid past to reveal. You must wonder why an earl would involve himself with such seedy characters."

Noel reached across the table and wrapped her hand over Ravencroft's fist. "To protect your brother."

"Yes. And now I do what I must to protect you."

"Then explain your drawings and let me help you. We are in this together."

He laced their fingers together. "Have I told you today how incredible you are?"

Noel gave him an impish smile. "No, but I would love to hear more of why you hold that opinion."

Ravencroft winked at her. "It might take all day."

Noel looked around the cottage. "I have nowhere else to be."

He chuckled and drew her onto his lap. In between explaining the drawings, he stole little kisses and whispered in her ear how incredible he thought she was.

Noel drew the blanket over Gregory as he slept. When they moved to the sofa to discuss their plans of escape, he had yawned and leaned his head back. It hadn't taken long before his snores filled the cottage. She wondered if he had gotten any sleep throughout the night. Unwinding from his side, she eased him onto the pillows and lifted his legs onto the sofa.

After straightening the cottage, she decided to implement the next stage of their plan. They had disagreed about who should befriend the guard. What better opportunity did she have while Gregory slept? She had promised him she wouldn't make an attempt if he didn't stand guard, but she didn't see where it would hurt to at least try.

When she strolled outdoors, the guard stepped out of the shadows. She pretended embarrassment and pointed toward the trees. He grunted and turned his back on her. Noel took it as a sign of trust or he assumed she wasn't a threat. If so, that was his first mistake.

Noel stepped around the corner and walked to the rear of the cottage. She stopped after a few steps and searched for the secret panel. She undid the latch that would lead them to safety. As soon as Ravencroft woke from his nap, she would confess the last secret between them.

Noel hurried back to the front, wiping her hands along her breeches. She looked up at the sky and noticed the dark clouds. A cool breeze wrapped itself around her, and she shivered. "Would you like a blanket to keep warm?"

"No, my lady. You best get indoors if you finished taking care of your needs."

Noel's lips twisted. "But I feel horrible for the conditions you must endure."

The guard grunted. "'Tis my duty."

"That is my point. If you did not have to stand guard over me, you could be inside, enjoying a warm meal," Noel argued.

"Inside."

Noel frowned but followed his order. However, she returned with a blanket and a tin of cookies she had found in the basket. After placing them in his arms, she smiled at him and then returned inside, closing the door.

"Noel?" Across the cottage, Gregory sat up and raked his hand through his hair. He was a handsome devil. A complicated one, but handsome all the same. She could gaze upon him for hours on end.

"Did you have a nice rest?"

He frowned. "Where did you wander off to?"

"I needed to use the outdoors," Noel explained.

"Alone?"

"The guard is harmless, Gregory."

Ravencroft growled. "Do not underestimate what he is capable of, should you dare to cross him."

Noel waved her hand at him. "Nonsense. He is harmless."

Ravencroft fisted his hands, frustrated at getting his point across to Noel. She refused to see the severity of their situation. He must get her to safety before her naivety caused them any more problems.

"I have need of the outdoors now," Ravencroft stated before storming out.

Noel shook her head at the temper he tried to keep hidden and cleared the mess on the table. Then she prepared their plates for dinner. It was another meal of bread and cheese. At least they had apples for dessert. How she longed for a warm meal spent with her family.

Her family had never entered her thoughts since she read Graham's and Maggie's letter yesterday afternoon. Ravencroft had consumed her attention. She smiled because it was quite a pleasant feeling to have one's thoughts consumed by the one they loved.

Ravencroft stormed around the cottage, not even explaining himself to the guard. The woman was exasperating. Why couldn't he get her to understand the threat they were under? While he held pride that she had stood up to his mother, he also cringed because the outcome of her spirit would also be their downfall.

He stopped, crossed his arms over his chest, and surveyed the land before him. Was it possible for them to escape through the forest? Or would they find themselves caught in a fresh set of problems? They were out of options. Lady L declared her return in three days. But she had lied, which left them a day to escape. He would finish the drawings tomorrow and leave them as bait. Tomorrow evening, they would make their escape.

When he came around the corner, he noticed the tin sitting on the blanket by the guard's feet. He recognized them from the basket Lady L had left. Did the guard step inside while he was behind the cottage? He wanted to make demands but needed to win the guard on their side. It would appear Noel had already worked on charming the guard.

"Do you require anything else to help ease your comfort?" Ravencroft asked.

The guard glared at him. "Now, why would you be wanting to do that?"

"Because it is hospitable to offer since it will be a chilly evening," Ravencroft answered.

"You toffs make no sense."

Ravencroft shrugged. "I only sympathize with you. A word of warning, hide those provisions from the other guard and don't let Lady L catch wind of accepting those from the lady." He cringed. "I would hate for you to get punished because my lady offered you her kindness."

The guard grunted.

Ravencroft continued to play on Noel's act of generosity since the guard seemed more approachable by Noel. "My lady would be upset if they harmed you because of her generosity. She would suffer from so much guilt."

"Take the damned items back inside."

Ravencroft shook his head. "That would be an ungracious offense. No. My lady would assume I took them away from you. Plus, I share her sentiments by offering those to you."

The guard didn't answer. Ravencroft noticed how the guard pondered about what he said. He turned toward the road with his hands behind his back and rocked on his heels as if he shared a friendly conversation with a mate, not with a guard who had orders to kill them if they attempted an escape.

"I sure hope it doesn't rain before Lady L makes her return for us. I suppose if it does, we can make room for you inside."

The guard barked out a laugh. "The other blokes said you would try to lay on the charm with your friendly banter." He nodded his head at the door. "Get inside before they catch sight of you. You are going to cost me a quid."

Ravencroft narrowed his gaze. "What else did they say about me?"

This brought a huge grin to the thug's face. "What a fool you were."

"How so?"

"That you do not have a clue on whose cottage Lady L trapped you in. I will admit, it was brilliant of her. You see, toff, I only place my loyalty on those I admire because of their intelligence. Not with those who rely on others to make his path through life."

Ravencroft attempted to argue the point. "Lady L found an abandoned cottage and is using it to suit her purpose."

"Not abandoned. Just not used for a while."

Ravencroft snarled. "Who does it belong to?"

"Ask your lady. She knows."

The guard's laughter irritated Ravencroft. He stepped forward. "Who owns the cottage?"

The guard's lips twisted into a smile. "The lady's brother."

Ravencroft rolled his hand into a fist, ready to thrash the smile off the guard's mug, but he stopped himself. He unrolled his fist and entered the cottage, gritting his teeth so as not to unleash his fury on Noel. She sat at the table waiting for him, with a smile of innocence graced on her face.

While he had torn down his defenses and admitted to his faults, giving Noel his trust, she had clung to her trust, not allowing him an ounce of forgiveness. Every time he thought he had her figured out, she showed him another side of herself. He understood her vulnerability, but he had stripped himself bare and told her secrets he had never told another soul.

"You gave the guard a blanket," Ravencroft accused.

Noel smiled with patience at his tone. "And cookies."

"Why?"

"Because I hoped to win him over to our side."

Ravencroft scoffed. "Do you suppose he will abandon the coin Lady L has promised him because you offered him a blanket and cookies?"

Noel frowned. "I attempted to befriend him. You underestimate my power to do so."

He shook his head in disbelief. "Oh, believe me, *my lady*, I am learning to never underestimate you."

Noel stood up. "What are you implying, *my lord*?"

Ravencroft didn't answer her at first. He noted she took up a defensive stance and her calm demeanor disappeared. He weighed his words before he spoke. Doubt clouded his thoughts. Perhaps she wasn't aware her brother owned this cottage. He had explained to her how a man took his mistress somewhere other than their home. Which would explain why

Reese had abandoned the cottage. As much animosity as he held for Reese Worthington, he didn't believe the gentleman carried on an affair. Worthington only held devotion to his wife and child and would never cause strife in his marriage.

He took a deep breath and spoke as calmly as he could. "Do you have something you wish to share with me?"

Noel's nose crinkled in confusion. "Nothing of importance."

If he didn't watch her so closely, he would've missed the slight cringe she made when she answered him. Not to mention how she avoided his eyes. Proof of how she knew who owned the cottage—and how she didn't trust him. He'd been willing to give her the benefit of doubt, but he was a fool, as the guard stated.

Ravencroft stepped forward and pulled out her chair. "Then shall we eat?"

Noel watched Ravencroft out of the corner of her eye as they ate in silence. Guilt nagged at her conscience for lying to him. She didn't understand why she didn't confess. While he was outside, she had decided to tell him about the cottage and the secret entrance. As she listened to him talking to the guard, she had worried she had upset him by offering the guard the blanket. However, something else they discussed had troubled Ravencroft.

Noel would coax him out of his troubled mood after dinner. She would confess once they retired for the evening. What bothered her wasn't the lack of conversation, but how Ravencroft refused to glance her way. Not even a smile. It was as if she disappointed him.

It was best if he kept silent. If not, then he feared his harsh reaction would inflict heartache on Noel. Whenever someone stirred his temper, he could be most brutal with his words.

After they cleared away dinner, he lost the sunshine to work on the drawings. A chill had settled in the air with the approaching storm. He lit a fire and settled in the chair, contemplating his next course of action. With a glance out the window, he hoped the storm held off until tomorrow evening. His gaze shifted toward the bed where Noel had pulled back the covers.

She blew out the candle and crawled onto the mattress. "Gregory, will you join me?"

The fire crackled in the hearth, and the wind started blowing, causing the tree branches to slap against the cottage. He noticed Noel shiver and wanted nothing more than to keep her warm. But his pride would keep him away from her for the night. Until Noel could trust him, he must stay away from her.

"No. I will sleep on the sofa tonight."

Noel pouted. "Why?"

He stretched his legs out in front of him, folding his hands across his chest. "Because until I can earn your trust, then it is best we refrain from intimacy."

Noel sat up in bed. "You have my trust."

"Do I?"

"Yes."

He sat forward suddenly. "Then why have you made me look foolish?"

Noel slapped her hand on the mattress. "I have done no such thing."

"Yes you have," he gritted out between his teeth. "By not divulging your knowledge about how your brother owns this cottage."

"Oh," whooshed out of Noel.

"Yes. Oh." Ravencroft barked out a sarcastic laugh.

Noel crawled to the edge of the bed, holding out her hand. "Please come to bed and allow me to explain."

"There is nothing to explain. You have shown you hold no trust in me, and I understand. Please allow me time to myself to process this."

"But I do. I meant to tell you when you came back inside," Noel pleaded.

"I gave you the perfect opportunity, and yet you still kept the knowledge to yourself," Ravencroft argued.

"I was unsure of what you referred to."

Ravencroft hung his head. "You were quite aware of what I referred to. Can we please discuss this tomorrow after I have calmed down?"

Noel nodded and crawled back under the covers. She kept her eyes on Gregory. He never once raised his voice in anger, only stating how he wished to calm down. She admired how in control he was of his emotions, not allowing them to dictate his words, while she only held disappointment in herself for not trusting him sooner.

She watched him settle in the chair and close his eyes, but he didn't sleep. She longed to go to him, wrap him in her arms and plead for his forgiveness. Noel didn't realize that holding onto her secret would hurt him so deeply. But then again, everyone Ravencroft had ever cared for hurt him with their secrets. Darkness settled around them, and the fire offered only a little light. Not enough to see him. However, she didn't need to stare at him to feel his heartache. Heartache she had caused and would heal.

And she vowed from this day forth he would never suffer from it again.

Chapter Fifteen

D RACOTT SLINKED THROUGH THE alleys, slipping in between the shadows to keep hidden from the evil lurking around every corner. He tried losing the person who followed him but to no avail. The gentleman stayed behind him. He followed Ravencroft's directions, which led him near the docks in the East End. Now he only needed to locate the prostitute named Jane who catcalled hackney drivers. Then he would be close to finding Lady L's hideout. He had traveled down every lane nearby but still couldn't find the whore. He almost returned to the office when a familiar face walked along the storefronts.

His luck took a turn, and he followed his old friend. He wished the gentleman following him wouldn't observe his confrontation with Ren, but he didn't want to lose this opportunity to learn where they kept Noel and Ravencroft. He understood the dire need to find them this evening because of his familiarity with the timeframe Lady L held prisoners. Dracott shuddered to think what would become of them on the morrow.

As close as he kept to Ren, it wasn't close enough. She slipped from his grasp again. He retraced his steps, hoping to find her, when someone pulled him inside an abandoned building.

Dracott pulled the knife from his pocket, ready to attack, when he noticed Ren leaning against the wall, wearing a smirk.

"Yes, love has weakened your defenses."

Dracott growled. "You almost got yourself gutted."

Ren rolled her eyes. "Please. I could've sliced your neck and you wouldn't have even known who I was."

Dracott slid the knife back into his pocket and ran his hands through his hair. Ren stood correct, as always. With Falcone following him and his mind filled with images of what his brother and Noel endured, he didn't pay attention to his surroundings. He had been careless and owed Ren his gratitude for keeping him alive. If one of Lady L's men had noticed him, they would've left him bleeding out in an alleyway, ignored by the harsh element of everyday life in the slums.

"Where are they?" Dracott demanded.

"Tsk, tsk. Your mother may have never taught you any manners, but I had least hoped your wife tried. Should you not offer me your gratitude for saving your life?" Ren asked.

"Thank you." Dracott bit the inside of his cheek, fighting for patience. He wanted to rush Ren along into telling him where they kept Noel and Ravencroft captive, but his friend had her own agenda for this meeting. With a reluctance to play her game, he propped himself up against the wall, waiting for her move.

Ren bit her lip, unsure how to read Dracott. At one time, she had known his moods better than her own. He wasn't the same friend who had taught her how to survive in this dangerous world. Dracott held himself with confidence she only pretended to express.

She missed their friendship but refused to focus on the loss. Because if she thought too long on the issue, she would experience the heartache she had endured when she lost her parents, a pain she never wanted to suffer from again. Instead, she regarded him as another soul who flitted in and out of her life and hardened her heart once again. She must face the truth of how she only had herself to depend upon.

Her fanciful childhood dreams of a knight coming to her rescue to sweep her off her feet and declare his undying love floated away in the wind each day she continued to live in this hell. While she never thought of Dracott in those terms, his abandonment still stung deeply. She envied his newfound happiness, wishing the same for herself. However, the reality of life held a different outcome for her, one that demanded she keep her head out of the clouds and focus on what she needed to accomplish. Since she could no longer depend on Dracott's help, she had no qualms about using him to gather information.

Ren's gaze raked Dracott from head to foot. "I see you mended well."

Dracott nodded. "No thanks to your associates."

Ren pushed off the wall and wandered along the hallway. "They do not play fair, do they?"

Dracott followed her. "They never have."

She stopped and turned. "In their defense, they only seek the approval of their mistress."

"That bitch deserves no respect," Dracott snarled.

Ren took a step closer to Dracott, leaning in like she meant to kiss him. Instead she whispered in his ear, "And yet one has to admire what she has accomplished."

Dracott clasped Ren's wrist before she stepped back. He tightened his grip when she tried to get away. "You no more believe that than I do. Now state your demands and then tell me where I can find them."

Ren glared at him for not playing along and ripped her arm out of his grasp. She rubbed her wrist, surprised by

his spark of anger. Dracott was never one to lash out unle
provoked beyond the calm patience he held. "You mu
distract your brother-in-law from searching for me. I cann
follow through with my plans when I'm avoiding his attentio
I only pray that the man who is following you doesn't link n
disguises together and confront you over them. Falcone w
not stay silent about the connection."

Dracott sighed. He wanted to help Ren, but he must consid
Maggie's welfare before risking their lives for the impossibl
No matter what he said, Ren refused to walk away. Howeve
he would offer his help. "All right, I can help you on that from

Ren nodded before continuing her walk to the opposite si
of the building. Once she reached the door, she gave him
clue. "Ask your employers about their cottage in the country
With that, she slipped outside.

Dracott didn't follow her. For her best interest, he neede
to exit the same way he had entered, even if Falcone waite
for him. It was in Ren's best interest to keep the gentlema
from piecing together her identity. He would sacrifice himse
for the sake of their friendship. Maggie and her family kne
of his and Ravencroft's past involvement with Lady Langdal
However, they kept the secret within the family, only allowin
Ralston and Kincaid knowledge of the truth.

Dracott opened the door and took a step outside, bumpin
into Falcone. The marquess stood still, glancing up and dow
the alleyway in confusion.

Falcone grabbed Dracott's arm. "You are coming with me."

Dracott shook himself free. "Never lay your hands on m
again."

Falcone snarled. "While I am not one to touch guttersnip
I will tolerate it to bring you to justice."

Dracott scoffed. "You are a fine one to speak, considering th
activities you partake within the gutters."

"I recognized your lover that you followed. Does Lady Margaret know of your affair? If not, I shall take pleasure in divulging your true identity to the Worthingtons. After the Worthingtons banish you, I will ensure your brother isn't too far behind. You both seemed familiar when I met you, but I couldn't remember where I had seen you before. However, when you followed your piece of fluff, it all became clear," Falcone ranted as he followed Dracott.

Falcone's threats were the least of Dracott's worries. He feared for Ren's safety and didn't know if he could keep Worth away from her. Or if he even wanted to. Worth had the resources to protect Ren and keep her out of harm's way. Perhaps even convince her to give up her foolish notions. However, he must reach Worth to ask what Ren's clue meant. Would it lead them to rescuing Noel and Ravencroft?

Falcone stormed into the office behind Dracott, shoving him to the side to reach Worth before he did. He stood in the doorway, watching Falcone attempt to destroy him. It was almost comical, but still an unwanted distraction.

Falcone pointed his finger at him. "There are traitors in our midst that you are unaware of."

Worth leaned back in his chair, crossing his arms over his chest as his eyebrow raised in question at Dracott. "Is that so? Please enlighten me on who would dare to betray my trust."

Falcone started pacing back and forth between the desks. "When I arrived for dinner the other night, Dracott and Ravencroft seemed familiar, but my suspicion of them wouldn't reveal itself. That was, until I followed Dracott today."

"Then you remembered?" Ralston leaned against his desk.

"Yes, but only after I spotted him consorting with the enemy," Falcone gloated.

Eden sent Worth a worried glance, but he gave a slight shake of his head for her to stay silent. She wanted to defend her brother-in-law, but his identity was a sensitive topic they must keep secret. If anyone discovered Dracott's and Ravencroft's past, destruction would fall upon their entire family.

"Do you have anything to say to defend your honor?" Worth asked Dracott.

Dracott shrugged. "I spoke with a source to discover where they hid your sister and Ravencroft."

"Do you know where they hold them?" Eden questioned.

Before Dracott responded, Falcone scoffed. "His source? More like his accomplice. For years, Dracott and Ravencroft belonged to Lady L's pack of degenerates. They have made fools out of your family since you allowed them into your fold."

Worth stood up and pulled his suit coat on. "Lord Falcone, will you please see my sister home? I have urgent business that needs taken care of."

"But . . ." Falcone sputtered.

"We can finish this conversation after I have brought my sister home from that evil woman's clutches. I ask for your discretion until then."

"Are you taking his word over mine? He bloody well is drawing you into their trap," Falcone growled.

Worth pulled his sleeves down over his cuffs. His patience was wearing thin. "A chance I will take to find my sister. Now, please guarantee Eden's protection and escort her home. Then I can rescue Noel with peace of mind. Do you think you can protect Eden from coming to any harm?" The last of his order held a sliver of a threat behind it.

Falcone glared at Worth, but Worth never wavered from his stance. When he received no response, he turned his glare on Ralston, who stood next to his partner in agreement. Then at Dracott, who propped himself against the wall without a care in the world. Or at least that was the impression Falcone held.

He refused to glance at Lady Eden and the smirk she wore. They invoked his rage by ignoring his warnings about Dracott. He stalked out the door, not offering the lady his arm. Instead, he waited by his carriage for her to exit.

Eden hated leaving. She wanted to help but understood Worth's need to see her safely at home with the rest of their family. She would grant him this, but after Noel returned home, she wouldn't sit by and idly wait for Worth or Ralston to hand her assignments. Eden wanted to help capture Lady Langdale and bring her to justice.

She kissed her brother on the cheek. "Bring them home. Alive." She continued on to show the same affection to Dracott. "Watch over him."

She walked outdoors to find a disgruntled gentleman pacing by his carriage. Eden shook her head at having to deal with his fury, but she would do so to protect her family. Part of her wanted to gloat at how Worth had set Falcone in his place, but the other part of her worried if he would destroy their family with his knowledge.

"Shall we?" Eden nodded at him to open the door.

Falcone landed his glare on her, and she held her head high, refusing to flinch. His presence might invoke fear in others, but she only found it disturbingly annoying. She climbed into the carriage and prepared herself for the longest ride ever in the shortest distance traveled.

"Where are they?" Worth demanded.

"Do either of you own a cottage in the countryside?" Dracott asked.

Worth and Ralston exchanged a glance. They hadn't used the cottage during the past couple of years due to them expanding their business into a new building.

The glance his employers shared gave Dracott his answer. "Lady L holds them hostage there. I have no other information, only a sense of urgency that we must rescue them this evening."

"We will take my carriage to my parents' estate. Then we can sneak through the forest of trees to reach them. Do you think Noel remembers the secret entrance leading to the forest?" Ralston asked.

Worth opened the drawer and pulled out his pistol. "Yes. Noel remembers everything."

"Why are we traveling to your parents' estate?" Dracott asked.

"Because the cottage sits at the edge of my parents' estate. It used to be an old caretaker's home, and we converted it into an office when we first started our business," Ralston explained.

"We will head home and get Reese. You inform Kincaid of our plans, and we will meet at the road leading out of town in two hours. Keep this quiet from your wife. I do not want the ladies upset or hopeful that Noel is coming home until we have her," Worth ordered.

Ralston nodded. "And I will send a word of warning to Colebourne about Falcone. He will take care of keeping the gentleman silent."

Dracott held no clue how the Duke of Colebourne held the power to keep Lord Falcone silent from revealing his and Ravencroft's identity. But Maggie had taught him to place his trust in people he respected. And with family. Most families only wanted to love and protect you from harm. Dracott would place his trust with these gentlemen because Maggie did. He only hoped he didn't misplace it.

For his sake, as well as Ravencroft's.

Chapter Sixteen

NO MATTER WHAT SHE did, Noel couldn't coax a smile from Ravencroft. She made him breakfast, helped him with the drawings, and apologized more than once. But he remained withdrawn from her. She even tried her innocent wiles on him, and he ignored every subtle hint. Noel wanted to kiss his frown away and hear his moans of pleasure from her touch. Perhaps she should try her seductive wiles on him instead. Maybe it would entice him enough to react. Noel giggled at the thought and drew another frown from Ravencroft.

Ravencroft sulked like a disappointed child, but he needed to stand firm on resisting Noel. He must finish the drawings because they would attempt to escape this evening. A light rain had started the day, and the sky brewed a ferocious storm amongst the clouds. They must make a break for their freedom tonight. He had overheard the guards discussing Lady L's plan to return tomorrow, which proved his theory correct that she wouldn't give them until the end of the week.

Ever since Noel had awakened, she'd been a distraction. Not so much a distraction but a temptation he struggled to resist after each apology. Even now, she giggled, and he wished for her to share her thoughts. His resistance crumbled with each gentle touch she teased him with.

He leaned back in his chair, scrutinizing her. He didn't understand how she accepted their predicament with such calm. Most ladies would've annoyed him with their hysterics throughout the ordeal. But not Noel. She had befriended a guard and did an excellent job of it, too. He heard the guard's tone soften when Noel questioned him about his night. And her concern was genuine. If he hadn't searched for his mother and gotten involved with Lady L, would he not view life through jaded lenses? Or look upon everything with cynicism? He portrayed himself to the ton as a happy-go-lucky gentleman, but his raging emotions were the complete opposite.

"Tell me about the cottage."

Noel smiled. Ravencroft must have forgiven her. "Graham and Ralston own the property. They took use of it when they started their business to discuss their cases. They would hide their witnesses here, too. However, the past couple of years they only visited it for personal reasons."

Ravencroft frowned. "The cottage doesn't belong to Reese?"

Noel crinkled her nose. "No. Not quite Reese's taste. What gave you that opinion?"

He shuffled the drawings, not meeting her eyes. "No reason."

Realization dawned at why Ravencroft thought the cottage belonged to Reese. "Eww. What a dreadful image that brings about."

A chuckle slipped out of Ravencroft. "Yes, I suppose it would for you. I assumed it belonged to Reese since Lady L knew of the property. I thought perhaps they had visited it during their liaison."

"No. Which only shows how knowledgeable Lady Langdale is about my family's holdings and activities. How long has she planned her revenge?" Noel asked.

"Since your brother married Evelyn and Colebourne ran her out of town. Colebourne put a bounty on her head. However, she was too elusive and escaped, remaining hidden all these years, during which time she kept adding forces to her thievery ring. She has prepared to destroy your family and anyone who ever wronged her for a lengthy time," Ravencroft explained.

"All because Reese refused to marry her?"

"Also because the ton never accepted her when she married her late husband. Her pride is something fierce that she wears as a badge of honor."

Noel understood why Lady L felt offended by the biting tongue of society. Reese's marriage to Evelyn had saved her family from ridicule. If Reese hadn't married Evelyn, the ton would've made their family suffer for their father's sins. But since Evelyn was the niece of the Duke of Colebourne and Evelyn's family married well, the ton had accepted the Worthington family without fault.

"How far away from the city are we?" Ravencroft interrupted Noel's musings.

"Only about a half hour drive by carriage."

"Damn," Ravencroft muttered.

He threw his chair back and started pacing around the cottage. He had hoped they weren't that far away. They risked exposure if they escaped. However, they had no other choice. He wondered how far they could travel through the trees. Perhaps once they reached the edge of the forest, it would lead them to a manor on the outskirts of the city.

"We can take the path through the trees during our escape," Noel suggested.

Ravencroft paused, staring at Noel in disbelief. "Why have you kept this information from me? Were you ever going to share it?"

Noel walked over to him and gathered his hands in hers. "Yes. I was foolish not to confide in you earlier, especially after you stood by my side with your mother. In all honesty, I stayed silent because you confused me. You went from a doting fiancé to a scoundrel who overtook my senses. I didn't know if I should trust you or not. After witnessing you with Lady L and your mother, I grew even more confused."

"And now?"

Noel stared Ravencroft in the eyes. "I trust you with my life and my heart."

He didn't know how to react. Ravencroft had dreamed of hearing Noel's sentiment but had given up hope he ever would. However, now that she had declared her feelings, his fear kept him silent. He didn't want to profess his love for her in a dingy cottage while Lady L threatened their lives. He wanted to make a grand gesture when he declared his love. It was only fair, considering the selfish reasons he had pursued her to gain her brother's approval for marriage. He would promise his devotion once he returned her home safely. For now, he needed to learn about the cottage.

He pulled away, moving back to the table to finish drawing. "Thank you for granting me that."

Noel stood in confusion. She had professed her love for him, and his only response was his gratitude. Well, she hadn't exactly spoken "I love you," but still she implied she did. Was he still sore about how she had kept the cottage a secret?

Noel turned to watch him. Her lips twisted as she contemplated how to draw him away from the table and into the bed. Lady L would return soon, and she wished to spend her time in utter bliss, not frowning over Ravencroft's behavior. She decided to sprinkle a little of her past infatuations in with knowledge of the cottage. Noel had wanted to scratch out Lady L's eyes when she pretended she and Ravencroft had a relationship. Perhaps Ravencroft suffered from the same jealous affliction as she did.

"Are you almost finished?" Noel asked.

"Mmm. Nearly." Ravencroft never glanced up and continued to draw.

Noel strolled over to him and trailed her fingers across his shoulders before walking away. "My first visit to the cottage was when Graham and I helped Gemma to spend time alone with Ralston. Graham and I took a walk while Gemma and Ralston settled their differences."

Ravencroft turned in the chair, curious as to why Noel told him this story. He noticed the blush covering her cheeks and realized what had really happened on that visit. The color pink was very becoming on Noel.

"I thought Ralston quite handsome the first time I laid eyes on him. However, Gemma had already taken an interest in him. It was lovely to watch their courtship." Noel smiled, remembering how her friends' love for one another had overcome all obstacles.

Ravencroft shook his head and turned back to the drawings. He thought Noel meant to describe the path, but she only wanted to reminisce. He didn't care if she found Ralston quite handsome. Obviously, she would never betray her friend. Her story was pointless to listen to.

Noel's eyes narrowed at Ravencroft's disinterest. Perhaps she was the only one who suffered from jealousy in their relationship. "But then, every single gentleman the Holbrooke ladies married is handsome. Even their cousins Lucas Gray and Duncan Forrester."

Noel laughed as she remembered her crush on Griffen Kincaid. "But the one I found most divine was Griffen Kincaid. Besides his dreamy physique, he is most kind. During a house party at Colebourne Manor, we were partners for charades. He allowed me to act out the clues after I told him how much I enjoyed playing the game. Then he paid me a compliment that made my evening one I would never forget."

"He is an honorable gentleman," Ravencroft mumbled.

"But then my attention swiftly changed to Lord Falcone. I found him even more divine, and I enjoyed flirting with him." Noel sighed.

Ravencroft growled his displeasure at listening to Noel ramble on about the gentlemen who had caught her fancy in the past. While her taste with Ralston and Kincaid was understandable, he found her interest in Falcone offensive.

"However, I saw it was clear even then. Eden and Falcone will make an excellent match. The air sizzles between them with their attraction," Noel continued.

Ravencroft scoffed. "You are mistaken in that regard."

"No, I am not. Watch them and you shall see," Noel argued.

"Your sister cannot stand the gentleman. Whenever she sees him, she shoots daggers at him. Not to mention her sharp tone when she addresses him."

Noel waved her hand. "It is part of the opposites attract chemistry that brews between them."

"Falcone is not a suitable match for your sister. Nor was he for your infatuation all those years ago," Ravencroft growled.

Noel laughed again. "Why, it only seems like yesterday that I imagined him professing his love and asking for my hand in marriage."

Noel had pushed Ravencroft past his limitation to keep his anger in check. He flipped the chair to the side and strode over to her. His irritation at her for mentioning her past infatuations struck a jealous rage throughout him. The thought of another gentleman touching Noel, even if innocently, set him on edge. But listening to her reminisce about how her heart fell for another man tore at his soul. Shredded it apart in a vicious attack meant to destroy him.

Ravencroft pulled her in his arms and lifted her chin to ravish her lips. His lips devoured hers, breathing his soul into her and wiping away any other gentleman who might have lingered in her heart. His kisses were relentless with each stroke of his tongue against hers. Noel's soft moans helped to soothe him, but the ache consuming him had only just begun.

Her mother had taught her to never poke the beast because one never knew what the outcome might be. Noel had always found humor in the saying but still followed her mother's advice. However, she didn't follow the advice today, and now the beast had unleashed himself upon her. With each delicious pull of his lips against hers, the beast staked his domain on her heart. Her body. Her soul.

In between his dominating kisses, he stripped the clothes from her body, leaving her bare to his gaze. She should feel vulnerable, but she only felt like a warrior princess who made her subject aware of her need. When his hand stroked along her body, claiming her as his, she pressed into his touch, making her own demands.

The demanding force to satisfy his cravings for this intoxicating bundle of innocence, seductive temptress, loving lady before him clouded Ravencroft's focus. His need blinded him, and he didn't notice her smile of satisfaction. She controlled him with her need to have him love her. Ravencroft thought he held all the power, but he was only a servant under her control.

His gaze raked her form, and each curve teased him by the way they dipped and flared at his touch. His hand reached out to caress them, sinking into their softness. With each caress, Noel arched her body, directing him where to touch her next. When his hands cupped her breasts, molding his hands around them, her soft moans filled the air. But then he remembered her naming a gentleman who had struck her fancy and his fingers tightened around her nipples, twisting until her moans turned to gasps.

With his own devious smile, he bent his head to draw them between his lips to soothe them with his tongue. Noel melted in his arms with each lick swirling around the hardened bud. Until his teeth scraped against the bud and his lips tightened, sucking harder.

"Gregory," Noel gasped, clutching at his shoulders.

Listening to his name on her lips helped to soothe his battered ego. But it still didn't heal the sting of how she might've given her heart to another.

Gregory sent her senses whirling from melting under his touch to craving a need only he could fulfill. He tormented her with each gentle caress and each dominating stake of claiming her heart. She provoked him in this exquisite torment and prayed he never stopped.

When his hand dipped below and slid between her thighs, stroking across her wetness, Noel's knees gave out. Gregory caught her and carried her to the bed. Her body craved more than his touch. While she had only set out to tease him to love her, she was unprepared for how much she needed him.

Gregory stared down at Noel, her gaze clouded with desire. His desperation to be the only man she ever thought of led him to this point. He could declare his love and ask her to promise him to never mention her past loves. But he wasn't a man to let softness rule his actions. At one time he had, but throughout the years, life had hardened him into this soul he existed in. If they were to share a life together, Noel needed to understand he wasn't the pushover gentleman she thought she had engaged herself to. He was a man jaded by the uncertainties of life.

Gregory tore off his clothes and crawled above her. He didn't need to prepare her before he staked his claim. When he touched her, her cunny had dripped with her honey dew. He drew her leg over his hip and entered her with the force of his need. Noel gasped and closed her eyes, throwing her head back and arching her neck. He pulled out and pushed in harder. Her fingers dug into his arms as she held on.

At her every movement, his need for her grew. Each time he pounded inside her, she drew him in deeper. Each gasp pushed him to move faster. Each glide of his cock into her wet pussy hardened it to an unbearable ache. He refused to release his desire because he needed to settle into the bit of heaven she provided. When her body met his thrust for thrust, their souls twisted around one another.

Noel held no clue when her body had melted into Gregory's. She only knew the passion consuming them filled her heart and soul with an emotion she had no words to express. After this, there was no return to the emotionless souls who existed only because of their fear of heartache. No. They must face the hardships and embrace their emotions with the wonderment before them.

Gregory's desires unraveled out of control, and she needed to calm his battered ego she had set off with her mindless chatter about other gentlemen. Her fingers loosened their grip and slid along his arms in a gentle caress, while her body slowed her movements alongside his. She pressed her lips against his, murmuring about how he made her feel. His movements slowed with hers. Only each thrust hit her deeper in her core, spinning her passion back out of control. Her body begged for him to send her spiraling over the edge, yet at the same time, it pleaded with him to never stop its sweet torture.

The last of his control slipped away when she slowed her movements. He gripped her chin and growled. "You will never mention the name of another gentleman who you admired in my presence ever again." He slid his cock inside her achingly slow and pushed in deeper before pulling out and waiting. "Do I make myself clear?"

Noel hung suspended in the air with her need remaining unsatisfied, but it was within her reach if only Gregory would settle inside her again. The ferocity of his question broke her heart at how she had wounded him with her callous words. However, nothing prepared her for the tortured emotions expressed in his eyes when thunder exploded outside and lightning flashed inside the cottage.

The fear of her not loving him clouded his gaze. She never noticed Gregory's hand trembling on her chin because the passion had swept her away.

She wrapped her hand around his. "Perfectly clear because I love you. I am sorry—"

Before she finished, Gregory stole her breath away with a kiss that was filled with such emotion she wanted to cry. Instead, she kissed him with all the love she held for him in her heart.

Her declaration of her love sent him over the edge. He couldn't bear to hear her apology when it was he who needed to apologize for treating her like a beast. All it took was her sweet kiss to explode with his need. He grabbed her hips and sank into her as deep as he possibly could. Gregory forged the bond that entwined them into an impossible knot, holding them bound as one.

A bond for all eternity.

Chapter Seventeen

AFTER NOEL'S HEART CALMED to a steady beat, she rolled on top of Gregory. Her fingers fluttered through his hair. Her only thought was to help ease the torment that ravaged his soul. She wished he had never suffered as he had. However, it had shaped him into the man he was today. A man she wished to spend an eternity with. Now, she only needed to convince Gregory he was that man.

Noel attempted another apology. "It was wrong of me to tease you."

He pulled her hand away from his head. "No. I am sorry for making love to you like a barbarian."

Her lips drew into a smirk. "I quite enjoyed it."

Ravencroft frowned. "It was still wrong of me, and so was my temper. You may hold feelings for another before we met. I informed you of my past affairs, and I am sure you found those unpleasant to hear. I should've been mature enough to listen about yours."

"But I held no tender regard for any of them. I was a country miss who hadn't spent time with any gentlemen. Then I learned I enjoyed the art of flirting after my first season." Noel frowned. "Now that I remember correctly, the gentlemen only found my flirting a nuisance they wished to avoid."

"I am a selfish bastard who wished you only ever held tender emotion for me and no other gentleman." He kissed her knuckles.

Noel lifted her other hand and smoothed away the crinkles around his eyes as he frowned. "You are the only soul I have ever fallen in love with."

She pressed a soft kiss on his lips before snuggling against his chest. She didn't care how he never returned the sentiment. Gregory expressed his love in the way he treated her. She understood his hesitation to open his heart to her and how he didn't express his love lightly. Noel would remain patient and wait until the day he would.

They lay there, listening to the pitter-patter of the rain on the cottage's roof. The storm had yet to begin, but lightning lit the sky, announcing its arrival. Only a sliver of light peeked through the window. She must confess the cottage's secrets. Before long, their time together must end. Noel only hoped once they returned, Gregory didn't retreat into the false gentleman he had perfected before Lady L kidnapped her.

"A secret door rests along the back wall. I have unlatched it from the outside. We can escape through it and take the path through the forest to safety."

Ravencroft stiffened at her news. They could've made their escape already, but Noel had kept this information to herself. Why? Was it her lack of trust or for another reason altogether? Did it even matter anymore?

"Where does the path lead to?"

The rumble of his question vibrated against her chest. "The Duke of Theron's estate."

"Ralston's parents?"

Noel nodded, wincing at the news she had shared. She waited for Ravencroft's fury at her for staying silent about the most important detail of their escape. However, he only released a deep sigh that she couldn't decipher, and she was a coward by refusing to meet his gaze.

"We need to get dressed and prepare for our escape." He pulled away from her and donned his clothing.

Noel sat up in bed, drawing the sheet over her body. "Where are you going?"

Ravencroft stopped at the door. "We haven't been outside all day. I need to show the guard nothing is amiss. This will allow us to escape before they get suspicious."

"All right."

Ravencroft walked outside, resisting the urge to make love to Noel one last time with the gentleness she deserved. He wanted to love every inch of her, taste her sweetness, while his hands sank into every soft curve of her tempting body.

The guard barked out a laugh. "Coming up for air, are ye?"

Ravencroft cocked his head to the side. "Excuse me?"

The guard smirked at Ravencroft. "I listened to you swiving the missus quite good. She is a screamer. Should have known with how sweet she acted. The sweet ones always enjoy it a little rough. Wonder if she will scream that loud when I plow between her thighs."

Ravencroft only saw red. The emotions he had kept in check since Noel's kidnapping exploded inside him. With a roar, he lunged at the guard and sent them flying to the ground. The punch he threw slipped off the guard's cheek from the wet rain. But the guard's punch landed in his gut, taking his breath away. He rolled over, clenching his side. Each breath he drew was a soft hiss of pain. But the guard was far from finished with him. He picked Ravencroft up and delivered a right hook across his cheek, splitting his lip.

Ravencroft tasted blood seeping into his mouth when he took his next swing. He punched the guard in his eye and knocked him back. This only pissed the guard off, and it was no longer a fair fight but a pounding that left Ravencroft swaying on his feet after every punch.

"Stop it! Stop it now!" Noel shrieked over the thunder.

She moved in between them, forcing both of them to drop their arms. The guard picked up Noel with ease and planted her by the door.

Noel issued a warning before the guard finished Ravencroft off. "If you do not stop, Doyle, I will not fulfill the promise I made to you. Or perhaps I should inform your sweetheart of your ability to act violently against another soul."

Whatever Noel had promised the brute, it was enough to make him stop advancing on Ravencroft. Noel noted this and came to his side, wrapping her arms around his waist and leading him back inside to the bed. He leaned back and closed his eyes, fighting against the pain racking his body.

The mattress dipped when Noel joined him on the bed. A soft cool rag gently brushed over his sores. She whispered soft words of reassurance as her lips followed the path of her tender care. When he opened his eyes, it was to stare into her confusion.

"What happened?" Noel whispered.

"Nothing." He attempted to rise, but a sharp pain stabbed him in the side, hindering his movement.

"Will we ever have honesty between us?" Noel's question gutted him.

He longed for honesty to rule their actions toward one another. But dishonesty ruled his world, and he had forgotten how to speak the truth. Truth was an illusion that ceased to exist. He wished to share the truth with her. However, some truths were meant to stay hidden. The brute's slander of Noel was an insult he'd take to the grave. He refused for her to suffer embarrassment over the crass talk and withdraw into herself. She only blossomed when she embraced her sensual being.

Ravencroft rose after the pain had lessened. They needed to leave now before the other guard came to finish him. He refused to allow Noel to be vulnerable in their care, especially after the guard expressed how he wished to defile Noel.

"Only part of my plan, love, to keep them from checking in on us." Ravencroft's lie slipped off his tongue so easily. Only he cringed with each word he spoke in dishonesty.

Ravencroft rose and set the scene for their departure. He lit a fire in the hearth and propped the pillows underneath the blanket to make it appear as if they slept. Noel stood in indecision with her hands on her hips, watching him. She slipped on her shoes and waited near the back wall for him to join her once she believed he told the truth.

He debated if he should keep candles burning but decided against it. Worth had stressed how important it was for Lady L to take the drawings into her possession. If a candle fell and burned the cottage to ashes, then his efforts to bring her to justice would be for naught. He kept a candle lit while Noel explained the door to him.

"When they used the cottage to help protect their clients, they installed this secret door in case the client would need to leave undetected."

Ravencroft ran his hand over the craftmanship. Whoever had designed the door was brilliant. He had never noticed how the panel blended in with the woodwork. Noel pressed the secret latch, and the panel opened to their freedom. Rain splattered inside, hitting their legs. They must not leave any trace of the rain or the guards would realize how they escaped.

Ravencroft blew out the candle. "You go first."

He lowered her to the floor, and she slid outside. Noel's hand reached inside to help pull him out. He slid out on his stomach. The opening was a tight fit to accommodate his size, which left him to wonder who Worth and Ralston's clients were. Someone had designed the secret door for women or small children.

Once he got to his feet, he tried to lead them into the woods, but Noel held back, fiddling with the wood along the cottage. "We need to go," Ravencroft ordered.

An outpouring of rain off the roof landed on Noel. She wiped at her face, trying to explain. "We must secure the latch from the outside. Once the panel slides in place, the door locks from the inside."

Ravencroft nodded and helped her search for the latch. Once they secured the lock, he drew Noel's hand into his and headed for the trees. However, a shout rang in the distance, along with a carriage thundering down the lane to the cottage. The sky roared louder with its displeasure of the storm.

"Damn. We must hurry, Noel. We have no time to spare. Lady L has returned earlier than I predicted." He didn't give her time to respond and pulled at her to follow him.

"There is the path," Noel directed him.

They took off, swiping at the tree branches in their way. It wasn't long before he heard footsteps following them. Ravencroft started running, pulling Noel after him. The lightening flashing gave him glimpses of a path washed away from the rain and fallen branches to maneuver around.

"How far to the estate?"

"I do not remember," Noel cried.

He wanted to ease her fear by pulling her into his arms and reassuring her they would be fine. But he couldn't. He must forge them ahead and pray they didn't have far to travel. If they reached the estate before the guards, then Ralston's father would provide them with the security they so desperately needed.

Ravencroft released his hold on Noel when they came upon a fallen tree. He climbed over the barrier and reached back for

Noel. The guard stationed by the road was getting closer. He lifted Noel over the tree and ran. But Ravencroft slipped on the mud and fell down a small hill. Noel was in tears but kept on fighting. She crawled to her feet and reached for his hand.

"Run!" Ravencroft yelled.

Noel glanced over her shoulder and panicked when the guard grabbed at her. She took off running for her life. She evaded his grasp and darted in between the trees to lose him. Noel hid behind a tree, gasping for air while he taunted her with slanderous comments.

"Come here, missy. I only want to play."

Noel peeked around the tree and saw him facing the other direction. She only had to take off, but fear kept her frozen. Her fingers dug into the bark of the tree, the roughness scraping across her soft skin. She urged herself to run. Desperation clawed at her to move, but her feet stayed frozen.

"I wonder if I can make you scream like Ravencroft did when he plowed into you. Heard your screams clear up by the road. He always did plunder the ladies until they cried out with mindless screams of pleasure."

The guard's last comment wiped away every ounce of fear she held, only to replace it with fury. She wanted to scratch his eyes out. Then hit him over the head with Cook's heaviest pot.

"You fool! Run!"

Noel whipped around to see the young girl from Lady L's standing in the rain, ordering her to run, instead of informing the guard she had her in sight. Noel didn't question the girl's motives and took off running in the estate's direction. Or what she believed to be the correct path. She had lost her way in the rain with all the distractions.

The girl stepped out from behind the tree, crying out. Noel moved behind another tree to watch.

The guard saw the girl and yelled, "I've found her."

Doyle came upon them and yanked the girl up by the scruff of her shirt, leaving her dangling in the air while his gaze searched the forest. He gave a nod for Noel to run after he found her hiding behind the tree.

"That you have. Take her back to Lady L, and I will look for Ravencroft," Doyle ordered.

With the threat of them capturing her, Noel ran as if the demons of hell were on her heels. She looked over her shoulder, but no one followed her. However, she wouldn't feel safe until Ravencroft held her in his warm embrace again. Noel didn't know where to find him and didn't want to risk Lady L's guards capturing her. Nor would Ravencroft want her risking her life for him. So with each foot slipping out from underneath her, she ran to safety.

She swiped at her drenched hair to take notice of the lights in the distance. She cried in relief when the outline of the Duke of Theron's estate came into view. Noel dropped to the ground in exhaustion after a familiar face appeared before her. Her body shook from the sheer grief of her fear. The terror of her kidnapping overwhelmed her.

"Noel?" Gentle hands picked her up and carried her. She wrapped her arms around Kincaid's neck and clung to him. Her tears mixed with the raindrops, sliding down her face. "You are safe." His words were meant to calm her, but they only opened the floodgate of her emotions.

When they reached the parlor, he tried to set her on the sofa, but she whimpered and clung tighter. She never noticed his discomfort or the glances he shot to the side. All she noted was his kindness, a gift she could never repay but would accept because she had reached the haven of her family.

"Noel, honey, why don't you let Griffen go so he can finish his search?" Gemma Ralston, Noel's closest friend, urged.

Her cousin and Griffen's wife, Jacqueline, stood by her side, holding out a blanket.

Noel released her hold. "My apologies."

Kincaid tipped her chin up. "Never apologize to a friend. I am glad you are safe."

Noel nodded, climbing off his lap. Jacqueline drew the blanket around Noel, and the ladies urged her away.

After her initial fear subsided, Gemma's words came back to her. "Ravencroft?"

Gemma turned her around. "He is safe, too."

Noel took a step toward him. He turned his back on her but not before Noel noticed the pain reflected in his gaze. She gasped as she looked at Kincaid, then at Ravencroft. However, before she could explain, Ravencroft stalked away.

"Gregory?" Noel's voice wavered with uncertainty.

But he never stopped. He followed the rest of the men outdoors. He misunderstood. She needed him to understand how she hadn't been in her right mind when she allowed Kincaid to comfort her. It meant nothing but a friend's reassurance. Her breath hitched again and again. She couldn't breathe. Ravencroft's heartache drew her under. Finally, her tears burst forth and racked her frame.

She doesn't remember her friends helping her up the stairs and into a bedchamber. They helped her bathe and wash her hair, then sat before the fire, taking turns brushing her hair after helping her into a gown. Never once did they try to reassure her with false promises. They only held her, offering their love of friendship.

"My apologies, Jacqueline. I never meant . . ."

Jacqueline enfolded Noel's hands into her own. "As my husband stated, there is no need to apologize amongst friends. Not only are we friends, but we are family, too. Who else to cry out your fears and heartaches to?"

Noel sniffled. "I do not believe Ravencroft holds the same opinion. I fear I have given him doubt."

"Nonsense. His jealous pride will heal once he realized you weren't coherent enough to know who even held you," Gemma reassured her.

"You do not understand. While Lady L held us captive, I tried to spark his interest by telling him about my crush on Kincaid all those years ago."

Jacqueline winced. "That was not wise, my dear."

Gemma giggled. "I can only imagine his reaction."

Noel blushed a fiery red. She might as well finish out her story with them, so they could understand why she had hurt Ravencroft by accepting Kincaid's affection. "I also might have mentioned how divine I thought Ralston was after I first laid eyes on him. And then how my infatuation changed from Kincaid to Falcone." Noel winced. "I might have embellished my story about Falcone with mentions of how I dreamed of him offering for my hand in marriage."

"Oh dear," Jacqueline muttered. "Now I understand his reaction for what it was. You, my friend, must convince him otherwise." She paused. "That is, if you want to. Just because Lady Langdale forced you alone with Ravencroft and the gossip mill is spreading its rumors does not mean you have to accept him for your husband. Even if you were engaged before all this mess happened."

An impish smile spread across Gemma's cheeks. "Oh, she wants to, dear cousin. Look at the blush spreading across her cheeks."

Noel lifted her hands to her cheeks, hoping to cool them off. "I love him. There are so many layers to him, hiding his true character. He hides them deep within, where no one can see the honorable gentleman he truly is. It took an unstable lady to keep me hostage for me to discover who Gregory Ravencroft really is. And he is a gentleman who has claimed me, body and soul. I wish to spend the rest of my life showing him how much he deserves my love."

"You had an enlightening week in the cottage. I told you it held magic," Gemma gushed.

"Would you like me to explain to Ravencroft?" Jacqueline offered.

Noel shook her head. "No. I will. But thank you, both of you, for everything."

Jacqueline stood. "We are happy you have returned unharmed. I will go check with Griffen for any news."

After Jacqueline left, Gemma urged Noel to lie for a spell. They would wake her if they learned any news. She even offered to hold Noel's hand until she fell asleep. Her caring friends were a fortunate blessing.

But her heart ached to have Ravencroft by her side instead.

Ravencroft stood over Noel, watching her sleep. Her body curled into the pillow she clung to. He eased her fingers apart and brushed the hair from her face. But she didn't stay settled. Little whimpers escaped her throat, tearing at his heart. He wished to crawl next to her and hold her until all her fears subsided. However, he resisted what his heart wanted most of all.

She had made her feelings clear when she clung to Kincaid, instead of allowing Kincaid to place her in Ravencroft's arms. Even though she would never cause a rift in his marriage, she still held tenderness for the gentleman. What he thought they shared in the cottage was only an illusion he had tricked himself into believing. Lady L had forced them together, and that had resulted in Noel depending on him. She was presented with no other choice.

However, she did now. He would speak with her brother and release himself from the engagement for her benefit. He figured Worthington would jump at the offer since he didn't believe Ravencroft was worthy enough to marry his sister after learning of his past. And he couldn't blame him in the slightest. Because he would do the same if he had a sister.

With one last lingering look, he left her alone. However, Noel was never truly alone and never would be.

Unlike him.

Chapter Eighteen

NOEL ROLLED OVER AND reached for Gregory, only to find the bed empty once again. She opened her eyes to search the cottage for him but found herself surrounded by luxury instead. The previous evening came flooding back, and she closed her eyes to escape the memories. However, they would remain ingrained in her thoughts forever.

She rolled to her side and sighed at the sight of her brother watching her. Noel pulled the blanket over her head to hide from his observant gaze. But her brother was her favorite tormenter and yanked the blanket out of her grasp.

Graham quirked an eyebrow. "Not who you were expecting?"

"No." Noel didn't even try to deny she had expected someone else. Worth was also her greatest confidant and would offer his support however she wished him to.

"They offered him a room, but Ravencroft stated how he desired to sleep in his own bed. Then he requested a ride home with Kincaid."

"Oh." A tear leaked from her eye. He hadn't even inquired about her well-being.

"However, I saw him slip into your bedchamber before he left."

Noel slid up to rest against the headboard. "He did?"

Graham nodded. "Does Reese need to obtain a special license?"

Noel blushed and glanced down to pick at the blanket. On this topic, she would stay silent. She wouldn't share information about the time she had spent with Gregory with anyone.

Graham stretched out his legs. "I'll take your silence as a yes. However, after your fiancé's swift departure last night, it leaves me to wonder if he will be as agreeable. Would you care to explain, dear sister?"

"A slight misunderstanding," Noel muttered.

"Hmm. I only inquire because he became a crazed man when we held him back from entering the forest to search for you. When you appeared at the edge of the forest, he started for you but stopped when Kincaid picked you up. Kincaid tried to pass you into Ravencroft's arms, but you clung to Kincaid as if he were your savior. Even when Ravencroft rasped out your name, you wouldn't release your hold. The poor bloke holds my sympathies."

She didn't remember Kincaid trying to pass her over to Ravencroft because despair had overwhelmed her into a distraught soul. After listening to her brother describe her actions, she understood why Ravencroft had walked away from her.

"Did he injure himself?" Noel asked.

"Nothing that will not heal. Do you know how he received the nasty bruises covering his face?"

"An altercation with a guard before we escaped, protecting my honor," Noel explained, now understanding the beating Ravencroft had endured for her. "And Lady Langdale?"

Graham sighed. "By the time we reached the cottage, she had escaped. At least she took the drawings. Now we have an advantage over her."

"Will she trust them?"

"She has no other choice. She will go underground again until she is ready to seek her revenge." Graham stood. "If you are ready, Reese and Dracott are waiting to return home. If not, Gemma has offered to stay until you are ready to leave."

"Is Reese horribly upset?"

"Livid." Graham's eyes twinkled. "But he is grateful for your safe return. So enjoy the time he grants you to soak up his sympathy before he delivers his lecture."

Noel stood up and hugged her brother. "You are the best."

He returned her hug, squeezing her. "Please, I beg of you to never scare me again."

"I promise," Noel whispered.

"Also, I stand by your decision. Even more so after his act of bravery to bring you home to us. Whatever you require from me to convince him of your love, I will help," Graham swore to Noel.

She pulled back. "Even if I request your help to sneak over to see him again?"

Graham moaned. "Even that. Now hurry, brat. You know how Reese acts after he is away from Evelyn too long."

Noel giggled as her brother left. She dressed in a gown Gemma had left for her to wear. She sighed as the silky fabric caressed her soft skin. After a week of wearing breeches and the coarse shirt, she enjoyed the simple pleasure of the dress. She never wanted to dress like a boy again.

With her future shining brightly before her, Noel's heavy heart felt lighter from when she fell asleep. Leave it to Graham to show her how every obstacle led her along a different path. A path of happiness leading to the only true love of her life.

She only hoped Gregory felt the same.

Ravencroft had turned stark raving mad after a day without Noel. His every thought filled with images of them together. Her fragrance still clung to him, even after soaking in a bath. Noel haunted his dreams when he fell asleep. How would he survive another day without her?

He had waited outside on his terrace for the return of their carriage, then he called on Worthington without running into Noel and offered to withdraw his engagement contract. Worthington never argued against it. The earl could've forced Ravencroft to marry Noel due to how he had ruined her.

Instead, Worthington had only stared at him and stated, "If that is your wish, who am I to deny you? It is probably for the best since Noel deserves a man who is worthy enough for her love. And obviously, that is not you, Ravencroft." Then Worthington had the audacity to dismiss him with the sweep of his hand toward the door.

Ravencroft snarled at the memory. How dare that pompous arse state he wasn't worthy enough of Noel's love? He had bowed out of the engagement because Noel deserved better than him. He was dissolute in every form a man could be. A penniless man who seduced innocent victims for a depraved lady's agenda. A man so battered and bruised, he didn't understand what love even meant. He didn't even hold the ability to declare his love to the woman of his dreams. If Noel married him, she would realize what a mistake she had made soon after the wedding vows.

He looked at the bottle on his desk he had avoided all day. His dry throat begged for a drink of the tempting nectar. His thoughts begged for him to forget them. Ravencroft's heart bled for a taste to wipe away every emotion he held for Noel. He wrapped his fingers around the whiskey and lifted it to his lips. He closed his eyes as the warm liquid burned a path to his gut. Each lick of fire helped to soothe his troubled soul. After another long pull, he kicked his feet up on the desk. It might not wipe Noel from his thoughts, but it eased the ache of missing her.

After he drank half the bottle, his brother found him in the same position. However, he was slumped in the chair. He had discarded his cravat and unbuttoned his vest and the top of his shirt.

Dracott shook his head in disappointment. "Is this how you wish to proceed?"

"Exactly," Ravencroft slurred.

Dracott pulled the bottle out of his brother's reach and settled into a chair. "That is not an answer."

"Exactly," Ravencroft repeated, smirking at his brother's disappointed stare.

"You have ruined an innocent lady. The gossip mill is making up stories of her ruination. Also, you have withdrawn your offer of marriage. And not once did you make the effort to call on Noel to see to her welfare," Dracott accused.

"Exactly." Ravencroft chuckled this time.

Dracott bit his tongue to keep back from laying into his brother. But as much as Ravencroft frustrated him, he saw how tormented his brother was. If it wasn't for him, Ravencroft never would have walked a path of crime, abandoning his moral code. However, Ravencroft had sacrificed himself. The least Dracott could do was to show his brother how people not only valued him but loved him, too.

He rose, changing his mind about staying. "I will give you today to drink yourself into oblivion. But tomorrow, I will return. We shall discuss your next course of action after you sober up. In which you will marry Noel. She loves you, and you owe her your love in return. Because no matter how much you deny yourself a chance at happiness, I will make it my purpose to convince you otherwise."

Ravencroft grabbed at the bottle and took another drink. He lifted the whiskey to his brother in a toast. "You can try."

Dracott leaned across the desk and smiled at his brother. "And I will succeed."

With that said, Dracott left his brother to drink himself to sleep. He would return on the morrow to make his brother see reason. A drunken Ravencroft would never listen to a word of advice. But Ravencroft with a hangover would listen. Only to be left to his suffering once he finished. Dracott rubbed his hands together as he returned to the Worthington townhome.

He would take immense pleasure in torturing his brother.

Chapter Nineteen

RAVENCROFT NEVER FELL ASLEEP. Instead, he moved outdoors to sit on the terrace, clutching the bottle in between his hands while he watched the sunset. His lips twitched in a smile at how he had irritated his brother. The dynamics of their relationship usually led to one of them wanting to strangle the other to get their point across. However, none of that was necessary for Ravencroft to understand the reason for disappointing Dracott. Because he held the same disappointment in himself.

As the golden hue of the sun sank deeper and the light grey of the evening came upon him, Ravencroft reflected. He was amazed by how swiftly the sun set and then stars soon flickered in the sky. It was the same change that happened in a person's life. One day, a person lived a simple life, only to have it altered beyond their comprehension. Then, once they settle into that life, it swiftly changed again. In the past, he had lived each day changing to suit the circumstances he had found himself in.

But once he met Noel, he had settled into what he thought was a safe and predictable existence. Yet, his past refused to stay in the past. It came barreling back, forcing him to change and adapt to circumstances beyond his control. However,

Noel remained solid. Someone he could depend on. Well, that was, until he had discovered the passion between them. Its powerful force unsettled him like nothing before.

He tipped his head back to gaze at the stars. They reminded him of Noel. Sparkling. Shining. A spectacular sight to gaze at. The stars gave one hope of wishing upon them to make their dreams come true. Noel herself was a dream that haunted his sleep and invaded his every thought. One he wished to spend an eternity with.

He loved her.

And he was a fool for calling off their engagement.

Ravencroft grew still when the gate to his garden creaked open. He didn't need to look to know his visitor was Noel. A rush of joy spread throughout him. Her visit meant only one thing. He was the luckiest bastard in the world. Now, he must not ruin his chance at seeking her forgiveness.

"Not dressed like a ruffian tonight?" Ravencroft drawled once she came into view.

Noel pressed a hand along her dress. She swore she would never wear those clothes again, and she meant it. Plus, she wanted to entice Gregory this evening and wore a dress to show off her best features.

On her last visit, she had judged his mood right away. However, on this visit, his voice remained even, not showing if he cared. Dracott had mentioned Gregory was deep into the bottle again. She only hoped he remained sober enough for her to declare her intentions.

"Also, you are still noisy in your attempt to go undetected," Ravencroft baited her.

"Perhaps I wanted you to notice my arrival," Noel returned.

"Mmm."

Noel expected Gregory to say more, but he remained silent with his gaze focused on her. His eyes raked her form in a

LAURA A. BARNES

slow perusal. She walked a few steps closer to him. He lounged in a chair, his clothing in a disheveled mess. Dracott had mentioned how his brother was a drunken fool, and Noel had to agree. However, his eyes no longer held a haunted expression but carried a lightness she had never seen before.

Before she moved closer, Gregory rose and walked into his study. Noel frowned and followed him inside. She must have misinterpreted what she saw in his expression. Gregory had moved to sit behind his desk with his feet propped up on the wide expanse, still clutching the bottle of spirits. However, he never took a drink.

Ravencroft tipped the bottle at Noel. "Princess, you need to leave. Your reputation is in shreds from what I hear."

Noel stood with her hands on her hips. "No thanks to you. You owe me an explanation for abandoning me when I needed you the most."

He brought the bottle to his lips. The fiery nectar beckoned him to take a sip, but he pulled it away. "You appeared quite content with your hero of choice. Who be it for me to shatter your dream?"

Noel stomped her foot. "You foolish oaf. You are my dream. If you possessed an inkling of empathy, you would've realized I wasn't in my right mind when I escaped the forest."

Ravencroft shrugged. "Does it really matter? You are better off without me."

"You cannot believe that after what we shared. How dare you pretend what we shared wasn't real," Noel exclaimed.

Noel in a snit was a sight to behold. He didn't mean to bring his jealousy to light. But then, he supposed he wished for her to deny what he saw. Oh, how she tempted him with her lips drawn into a pout.

He dropped his feet to the floor and strolled to her side with a slow gait, watching her grow flustered with each step he drew closer. He wrapped a stray curl around his finger. "I dare because I can."

Noel's breath quickened. "You are the most irritating . . . infuriating . . . gentleman I know."

His thumb brushed across her quivering bottom lip. "You forgot to mention how irresistible I am," Ravencroft whispered before drawing her into his arms.

He never gave her a chance to respond before his mouth covered hers and ravished her lips in a kiss so profound it left both of them shaking. But he didn't stop at one kiss. He pulled one after another from her sweet lips. Each kiss was more intoxicating than the last. His thirst for her kisses would forever stay unquenched.

Since she arrived, Noel had questioned if she should return home. But once Gregory drew her into his arms and kissed her as if his life depended on it, her heart swelled with love. Once again, the wonderful sensation of being one with Gregory swirled around her. Her arms slid around his neck, and she melted against him.

Gregory lifted her and carried her to his desk, where he set her on it and pulled away. With a smirk, he sat back in his chair, staring at her. Her cheeks were flushed, and her eyes held the dreamy expression of happily ever after. But her body spoke an entirely different story. It displayed her desire for him.

Noel had arched her body with her hands sprawled out behind her. Her nipples had hardened, pressing against the light fabric of the gown the temptress had worn to seduce him. It was pure seduction with her neckline cut low enough for him to view her bosom pushed together. The globes beckoned him with their shiny glow. The rest of the dress hugged her curves, begging for him to caress them. Her skirt was long and flowing along her legs.

He drew one of her legs onto the arm of his chair and skated his hand along the delicious length, sinking into her soft thigh. All the while, he watched her expression cloud with need as his fingers glided across her wet core. God, she felt like heaven. A soft moan escaped her lips when he slid two fingers inside her. With each slide in and out, her moans grew louder, playing out a melody for his ears.

He had fantasized about her sprawled across his desk since she arrived uninvited, demanding he make right by her. His other hand drew her other leg onto the chair and pushed her skirts around her hips. Noel's eyes had lowered but were open enough to watch his every movement. He sat forward, slowly drawing his tongue along the sweetest cunny he had ever savored.

Noel sighed. "Gregory."

Noel had never felt more decadent, and it was the most amazing sensation ever. Gregory seduced her with each touch and kiss upon her soul. She arched her hips higher, earning a growl from him. It vibrated against her folds, increasing the sweet torment he strung out with his seduction. She slipped away to the heaven he led her to with each kiss.

She unraveled with each stroke of his tongue, and he got drunk off her sweet juices. No amount of whiskey had ever tasted this delicious. His tongue flicked her clit into a hard bud, building her tension higher and higher until she exploded around him. He smiled at the slight tremors shaking her body, taking pleasure in sending her flying to those heights.

Ravencroft sat back with a smirk. "Another lesson you achieved with fine results."

Gregory's smirk spoke volumes. When she set out to visit him, she had thought she would have to convince him how their love was worth fighting for. Oh, she knew he had yet to declare how much he loved her. But his every action since they escaped from the cottage proved it. When she arrived, he had baited her in the same manner he had on her first visit. But somewhere in between Dracott's visit and her own, he must have seen reason and only teased her. Well, he wasn't the only one who could tease.

Ravencroft knew he was at Noel's mercy when her lips lifted into a sultry smile. Her confidence as she rose from the desk and settled between his legs wiped the smirk completely off his face. When she undid the placket of his trousers and slipped her dainty hand to pull out his cock, he realized she meant to fulfill his proposition from her visit a week ago.

Her hand glided up and down on his cock, drawing out a moan from Gregory. Noel peeked out from between her lashes to see his reaction. His eyes darkened to a midnight blue filled with desire as he watched her. Her tongue struck out to lick around the tip before she sucked it between her lips.

Gregory groaned. "Holy hell, Noel."

Noel smiled as she drew him deeper into her mouth, her tongue swirling around, licking off his juices. Since the ton whispered about how she was a wanton hussy for stealing away with Ravencroft, she'd at least have the pleasure of making the whispers true.

Gregory's hands dove into her hair, guiding her head closer. Each time she drew him in deeper, his hands would curl into fists. Her tongue flattened and trailed along the length of his cock. He pulsed against her tongue with need. Noel drew the tip into her mouth and sucked down hard, her tongue flicking back and forth across the slit.

She pulled him out of her mouth, her hand stroking him up and down, and sat back. He growled his displeasure.

"Why?"

That one word held so many questions but also held the simplicity of one answer to satisfy her. "I was a fool."

Her tongue darted out to tease him. "Are you still one?"

Gregory shook his head, unable to form a coherent answer. He lost all sense of his sanity with her lips wrapped around his cock. She lowered her mouth over him, drawing him in with such agonizing slowness that it also held the most pleasure he had ever felt. When she pulled away, he wanted to beg for her to finish.

Her thumb ran across his wetness, coating it down the length of him. "Was that a yes or a no?"

"Yes." Gregory moaned. "No. Yes. No! I mean no."

Noel's tongue struck out along his length, savoring Gregory's wetness. She was horrible to tease him so. However, he must suffer for acting like a fool, and what sweeter way to torment him? "Which is it? Yes? Or no?

Noel devoured him again, sucking him harder with a relentless need, staking her claim on him. Heart and soul. Gregory's answer was music to her own soul with each no he chanted over and over. His body tensed, ready for his release, but Noel wanted him inside her. Noel wanted to soar with Gregory.

She slid up his body and gave him a kiss before pulling away. She smoothed her skirts down and walked to the door. Noel glanced over her shoulder, gave him a seductive smile, and took off along the hallway.

Where in the hell did the temptress go? He groaned at the ache consuming him, but he refused to finish himself off. Gregory tore off after her and found her sitting halfway up the stairs, leaning back on her arms. He climbed each step slowly until he reached her, his gaze ordering her to stay put.

Gregory's gaze scorched her with one burning lick of desire after another. His hands slid up her legs, pushing her dress around her waist. When his fingers sank into her wetness, Noel arched her body off the steps and into his embrace. Gregory's arm wrapped around her waist and brought her up against his hardness.

"Where are you going?" Gregory growled before he licked a path of fire along her neck.

Noel was only capable of murmuring, "Bedroom."

Gregory left Noel gasping for air when he drove his cock inside her. "I do not believe we will make it that far."

Gregory pushed his cock inside of Noel as deeply as he could and rotated his hips, drawing out her screams of pleasure. She wrapped her arms around him, holding on while he drove their passion higher and higher. When her legs clung around him and she pushed her hips off the steps, he finally surrendered to the love she held for him and sent them soaring to the highest peak of ecstasy.

He leaned over Noel and drew her lips under his in the gentlest of kisses. She held the ability to send his passion to uncontrollable heights, spinning him out of control. He wanted to spend a lifetime worshipping her. But would she allow him to?

Gregory pulled back, lifted Noel into his arms, and finished climbing the stairs. When they reached his bedchamber, he set her on her feet and undressed her. A soft blush spread across her body, but she stood with confidence that only stroked his need to make love to her again. Soft and slow. Where he could spend hours kissing every part of her body before sliding inside her. Soft and slow

Noel couldn't take her eyes off Gregory. He treated her how one would care for a porcelain doll. Gentle and caring. After he removed her last piece of clothing, she helped discard his. Each button undone brought a kiss from her. Once she finished, he lifted her again and placed her in the middle of the bed. Then he made love to her so tenderly it brought tears to her eyes. Each caress and kiss was filled with his love. Gentle and caring.

They lay wrapped in a love so profound it healed their wounded hearts.

Chapter Twenty

RAVENCROFT AND NOEL HAD fallen asleep and awakened wrapped in each other's arms the following morning. Neither of them spoke but stared deeply into each other's eyes.

Gregory's hand stroked along Noel's shoulder and down her arm. "Will you forgive me?"

"There is nothing to forgive, my love. I understand why you spoke with Reese. It is I who needs to explain my reaction with Kincaid."

Gregory kissed the top of her head. "No, you do not. I was a jealous fool who overreacted, and I understand the terror you endured. The evening of our escape held a familiarity I had experienced before. However, it was one you had never suffered from. I owe Kincaid my gratitude for offering you his friendship."

Noel rolled over and propped her hands on his chest. "Will your jealousy continue to be an issue between us?"

Gregory quirked his eyebrow. "I don't know. Are you going to provoke me by mentioning another gentleman's name?"

Noel smiled. "Maybe . . ."

He rolled her over, kissing her slowly. "I do not deserve you."

Noel brushed his hair off his forehead. "Something you have mentioned before and will spend a lifetime trying to achieve."

He chuckled. "As I also said before, you're the devil's temptress sent to wreak havoc on my life."

"And you wouldn't have it any other way," Noel responded.

"No. I would not." He rolled back over, drawing her into his embrace.

"Will you make me a promise?" Noel asked.

Gregory squeezed her. "Anything."

"Whenever your emotions overwhelm you, will you speak with me first? Instead of putting up walls between us. I understand your doubts, but I do not want any secrets between us. Our secrets have created doubt with one another. I want honesty in every aspect of our marriage."Gregory sighed. Noel spoke about a lifetime together, and he had yet to tell her he loved her. Her acceptance of waiting for him to declare his love only made him admire her more. She gave him her heart freely, and it made granting her promise so simple.

"I promise. Over the years, I learned to not trust a soul, except for Dracott. But throughout the week, you taught me how to allow myself to trust someone as special as you," Gregory said.

He wanted to make a grand gesture when he professed his love. He wished to ask for her hand in marriage and to spend a lifetime creating a family while they rebuilt his home. But then he realized Noel didn't need a grand gesture. She only wanted him to profess his utter devotion.

He rolled her back over and saw how happy his promise made her. Stars glistened in her eyes. He smiled down at her, his heart bursting, ready to profess his love. "Noel . . ."

The door to his bedroom flew open before he could say anything. He covered Noel with his body, protecting her from the intruder. His house sat empty of servants. Did Lady L return to strike her revenge?

"Get dressed. They captured Noel again." Dracott threw the clothes off the floor at him.

Ravencroft released his breath and relaxed against Noel, keeping her hidden from his brother. "Get out. I will be downstairs after a bit."

"We don't have time for your idleness. Do you not care for Noel?" Dracott growled.

"Very much," Gregory whispered so softly only Noel heard him. "With all my heart."

Noel's breath hitched at Gregory's declaration. She wanted to tell him how much she loved him, but her sister barreled into the bedroom behind Dracott.

"What is taking so long?" Maggie saw Ravencroft in bed, naked from the waist up. "Oh. I see." She quickly turned, looking at the floor. Anywhere but at the bed. However, she noticed her sister's dress lying amongst Ravencroft's clothes.

"Dammit. Ravencroft, get your arse out of bed now," Dracott thundered. He was on the verge of losing all hope for his brother. Did Ravencroft not care about Noel? Either way, he owed the Worthington family his cooperation in bringing her home safely again. When his wife stepped closer to the bed, trying to peek around Ravencroft, he barked, "For God's sake, Maggie, stand back."

Maggie laughed. "Reese is not too far behind us." She waited until she heard her sister groan. "And Mama is with him." She turned around and tugged Dracott from the bedchamber. "Welcome to the family, Ravencroft. I believe I might like you after all. No one else can make Noel throw all caution to the wind."

Maggie closed the door behind them, and they listened to her laughter echoing along the hallway.

"Your sister is a menace. Remind me to buy locks for our bedchamber doors," Ravencroft muttered.

Noel giggled. "Yes. Maggie has an awful habit of walking in where she isn't invited. I suppose we'd better dress and join them below."

Noel slipped out from underneath Gregory and dressed. But he remained in bed with his arms folded behind his head. His intense stare made Noel nervous. She sat on the bed, pulled up her stockings, and tried to smooth out the wrinkles on her dress. But they refused to budge, and the fabric remained crinkled.

Noel cleared her throat. "Umm. Are you . . . That is . . ." She took a deep breath. It was one thing to act wantonly when they were alone. However, it was scandalous to remain alone with him while her family waited for them. And with Ravencroft naked, too. "Should you get dressed?"

Gregory pulled Noel back into his arms, nuzzling her neck. "In time."

"Ahh." Noel sighed, her family already forgotten.

He tipped her chin up, gazing into her eyes. "I love you, Noel Worthington. Will you do me the honor of becoming my wife? Before you answer, you must understand how I wish for you to help me rebuild our estate and for us to fill it with our children. To show them all about love and trust. And I refuse to return to the manner of engagement we held before. I want this one filled with passion, love, trust, honor, and most of all, forgiveness."

Tears leaked from Noel's eyes. They were not tears of sorrow, but tears filled with joy. She had waited with patience for him to speak of his love because she understood the heartache he had endured from his own parents.

"Yes. Yes! Yes!" Each of her answers grew louder. She wrapped her hands around his cheeks, staring into his eyes.

"I love you, Gregory Ravencroft, and I cannot wait to fill our home with our children. To spend every day showing you how much I love you. And believe me, this engagement will hold all you desire." She winked at him. "And then some."

Before Gregory laughed with his happiness, Noel devoured his lips. And it wasn't long after that he drew her underneath him and showed her exactly how passionately he wished their engagement to be.

Her family be damned.

Chapter Twenty-One

N OEL AND RAVENCROFT DESCENDED the stairs, holding hands to encounter their brothers standing at the bottom of the staircase. Reese and Dracott stood glaring at them.

While Graham rocked back and forth on his heels with a huge smirk on his face. "About time you joined us. I thought we needed to send Maggie back upstairs to interrupt your—"

"Graham, that is enough," Reese growled.

Noel stood on her tiptoes and placed a kiss on each brother's cheek before hooking her arms through theirs. She looked over her shoulder and winked at Dracott before leading them toward the sound of voices in Gregory's parlor. It would appear her family had made themselves comfortable in her fiancé's home.

Once she stepped through the entryway, she went over to her mother, kissed her on the cheek, and sat down next to her. She looked over at Maggie, Eden, and Evelyn and blushed at their smirks. "I am sorry if I caused you a fright."

All of a sudden, everyone spoke at once. Reese snarled his displeasure at finding his sister in a scandalous tryst. Graham, Eden, and Maggie teased her relentlessly. Evelyn only smiled at her with a sisterly love of her happiness for Noel.

However, her mother had remained silent, her gaze directed at Ravencroft. Noel shifted her gaze to find him leaning against the wall, watching the chaos of her family with amusement. He used to make his excuses to leave when her family acted this way, but today he seemed to enjoy it. It made Noel smile.

"I apologize for my family's invasion into your home, Lord Ravencroft. However, I am sure you understand the need for our frantic visit," Lady Worthington spoke, and everyone grew quiet, waiting to hear how Ravencroft would explain his actions.

He stood up straight and drew his hands behind his back. "It is I who should apologize for overstepping the bounds of my engagement to Noel."

"What engagement? You called off your offer. After we leave, you will cease all contact with Noel," Reese snarled.

Ravencroft walked over to Noel and held out his hand. "No, I will not. Noel has accepted my offer of marriage." "Never," Reese ordered.

"Do you love her?" Lady Worthington asked, ignoring her eldest son.

"Yes, my lady." He wrapped his arms around Noel's waist.

"Mother." Reese scowled. "He has ruined her, discarded her, and once again ruined her, all within a week."

Noel sighed. "He has not ruined me."

"An unmarried lady spending an evening alone in a bachelor's residence tends to lead one to assume a lady's ruination," Graham quipped.

"That is enough, children." Lady Worthington observed the glow on her daughter's cheeks and the loving glances she gave Ravencroft and knew her daughter had found her soul mate. Ravencroft himself couldn't take his eyes off Noel, making her want to sigh at his devotion. "Take a seat, children, so we can decide when to hold the wedding."

Noel let out a yelp of joy and hugged her mother. "Thank you, Mama."

"Promise me you will give him the love he has missed out on all these years," Mama whispered in Noel's ear, only for her to hear.

Noel pulled back and nodded. Her mother was a gentle soul who had endured a marriage filled with unhappiness. She had only ever wanted her children to marry for love alone. She even held a special place in her heart for the people who had married her children. For her to make Noel promise to love Gregory only showed the depth of how much her mother cared for him as her own.

They sat down and decided to hold an engagement party in a week and for them to marry two weeks later. Evelyn drew Reese to the side while he grumbled his dislike at everyone for overruling his wishes. After his wife reprimanded him, Reese came over to them and drew Noel into a hug, wishing her happiness, and shook Ravencroft's hand in an offer of acceptance.

"Gregory, I noticed when we arrived that your house sat empty," Lady Worthington stated.

"Yes. I let the servants take a leave throughout this drama. I didn't want them to risk their lives for my sake," Ravencroft answered.

"Very honorable. I always knew you would be," Lady Worthington said.

Ravencroft frowned. "Had we met before?"

Lady Worthington sighed. "No. But I knew your father. I am afraid I caused his marriage to fall apart."

Ravencroft and Noel exchanged glances. This must be the information his mother had taunted them with.

"How so, Mama?" Noel asked.

Lady Worthington blushed. "I am not proud of my behavior, but I must share this information. It holds consequences for when you must deal with your mother. I learned your mother and my husband carried on an affair. This was before I discovered his debaucherous lifestyle. I was a naïve wife who adored her husband and believed everything he told me. However, over time, I learned they were all lies. I caught them together and confronted them, but they only laughed at how innocent I acted. Your father found me crying, and I poured out the reason for my tears. It was years later when your father confided about your mother's multiple affairs and how she abandoned her family. He was so heartbroken, and I blamed myself."

Ravencroft shook his head. "The blame only lies with my mother. You are not at fault but a victim of their nefarious dealings. I compliment you on your strength in enduring the cruelty and raising outstanding children. I only hope I can do the same with our children." He raised Noel's clasped hand with his and kissed her knuckles.

Lady Worthington smiled. "I believe you will." Then she rose. "Come along, girls, we have much to do."

She clasped her arm through Noel's, making sure she left. As much as she wanted to remain by Gregory's side, she understood she couldn't. But it didn't mean they couldn't steal some time alone later. She winked at him and followed her family home.

Ravencroft smiled at Noel when she left. He kept his silly grin on his face, even after his brother punched him on the arm. A lightness filled his heart and all because of one spectacular lady.

"It is good to see you smiling again," Dracott commented.

"Noel gives me every reason to," Ravencroft said.

Dracott sighed. "Hell is still knocking on our door."

Ravencroft grimaced. "Yes. However, I will not rest until I burn her down."

"And every menace who works with her."

"May they all burn," Ravencroft swore.

Epilogue

"**I** TOLD YOU THEY are meant for each other." Noel slipped her arm through Ravencroft's.

She always needed to touch him. She couldn't wait until they were married, when she would touch and kiss him endlessly all day long.

Ravencroft shook his head. "You are delusional, my love. Look at how your sister glares at him. She obviously wants to scratch his eyes out."

Noel laughed. "Her actions are false. When no one watches, she trails her eyes over him with longing. And Falcone follows Eden wherever she goes. Sizzling attraction fills the air, even clear over here."

Ravencroft tugged her behind a set of columns. "What you are feeling is my desire to drag you away and seduce you with my kisses."

Noel wrapped her hands around his neck. "Why, Lord Ravencroft, your suggestion is quite scandalous."

He nipped at her neck. "But one my seductive temptress longs for."

She tilted her head back to give him better access. "She also longs for words of utter devotion from her fiancé."

"I believe I can arrange that if my fiancée will follow me into the gardens," Ravencroft tempted.

Noel gasped. "Are you trying to cause a scandal at our engagement party?"

Ravencroft drew her lips into a kiss to show her how much of a scandal he would cause if she didn't follow him. His tongue stroked across hers, and he bit at her bottom lip. "I want every day of our life filled with our scandalous love."

Noel sighed into his kiss. "I believe I can arrange that."

With a seductive smile, she tugged at his hand and led him into the garden where they shared a scandalous tryst full of gentle caresses, soft kisses, whispered moans, and tender expressions of their love.

It was a love that bloomed every day into eternity.

Read Eden & Falcone's story in
The Fiery Vixen

Want to join my mailing list? Visit
https://www.lauraabarnes.com/contact-newsletter today!

"Thank you for reading The Seductive Temptress. Gaining exposure as an independent author relies mostly on

word-of-mouth, so if you have the time and inclination, please consider leaving a short review wherever you can."

Desire other books to read by Laura A. Barnes

Enjoy these other historical romances:

Fate of the Worthingtons Series
The Tempting Minx
The Seductive Temptress
The Fiery Vixen
The Siren's Gentleman

Matchmaking Madness Series
How the Lady Charmed the Marquess
How the Earl Fell for His Countess
How the Rake Tempted the Lady
How the Scot Stole the Bride
How the Lady Seduced the Viscount
How the Lord Married His Lady

About Author Laura A. Barnes

International selling author Laura A. Barnes fell in love with writing in the second grade. After her first creative writing assignment, she knew what she wanted to become. Many years went by with Laura filling her head full of story ideas and some funny fish songs she wrote while fishing with her family. Thirty-seven years later, she made her dreams a reality. With her debut novel *Rescued By the Captain*, she has set out on the path she always dreamed about.

When not writing, Laura can be found devouring her favorite romance books. Laura is married to her own Prince Charming (who for some reason or another thinks the heroes in her books are about him) and they have three wonderful children and two sweet grandbabies. Besides her love of reading and writing, Laura loves to travel. With her passport stamped in England, Scotland, and Ireland; she hopes to add more countries to her list soon.

While Laura isn't very good on the social media front, she loves to hear from her readers. You can find her on the following platforms:

You can visit her at ***www.lauraabarnes.com*** to join her mailing list.

Website: https://www.lauraabarnes.com/

Amazon: https://amazon.com/author/lauraabarnes

Goodreads: https://www.goodreads.com/author/show/16332844.Laura_A_Barnes

Facebook: https://www.facebook.com/AuthorLauraA.Barnes/

Instagram: https://www.instagram.com/labarnesauthor/

Twitter: https://twitter.com/labarnesauthor

BookBub: https://www.bookbub.com/profile/laura-a-barnes

TikTok: https://www.tiktok.com/@labarnesauthor

Manufactured by Amazon.ca
Bolton, ON

31309546R00129